## What Others are saying...

"A heartfelt conclusion to the Tradewinds Series, *Promise Me Aloha* delivers a touching story about friendship and finding one's place, full of summer nostalgia, shave ice, and Hawaiian sunsets. The perfect vacation read. As a soon-to-be Maui resident, I found this book a sweet addition to my shelf."

~Caroline George, author of *Dearest Josephine* and *The Summer We Forgot* (HarperCollins)

"Another great book by Taylor Bennett. Promise Me Aloha is a perfect teenage summer read. I was quickly captivated by the story and fell in love with the characters. They are genuine, fun and quirky. The story was medicine for my soul. Though it's written for teens this old gal thoroughly enjoyed Taylor's newest tale. Make sure to get a copy for yourself."

~*Bonnie Leon - Author of One Hundred Valleys.*

Bennett invites us to consider the beauty of 'imperfect' *ohana* in this concluding story of the *Tradewind Series*. I dare you not to cry as Olive takes this next step with Brander, while treasuring her relationships from the past and learning from those in the present. The perfect conclusion to an already classic series and a must-read for any bride-to-be!

~*Tara K. Ross, author of Fade to White*

Reading *Promise Me Aloha* is like reconnecting with dear friends who share all of your sweetest summertime memories. Taylor Bennett's vivid descriptions, relatable characters, and fun dialogue bring this heartwarming story to life and make the book nearly impossible to put down. This next chapter in Olive's life may leave you craving a shave ice and a plane ticket to Maui, but more importantly, it'll remind you of the beauty and power of sacrificial love and the God who is with us through all of life's adventures.

*~Anna Schaeffer, YA author of All of This and Just One Thing*

"*Promise Me Aloha* draws the Tradewinds series to a beautiful (and romantic!) close. Bennett's attention to detail creates vivid descriptions that leap off the page, enveloping readers completely.

Writing the final book in a series carries with it the enormous pressure of readers' hopes, dreams, and expectations, and Bennett does not disappoint. The proposal is just the beginning: *Promise Me Aloha* perfectly describes the tension (and fun) that goes into wedding planning, all set on the sands of the island readers have come to love."

~Olivia Smit, author of *Seeing Voices* and *Hearing Lies*

# Promise Me Aloha

# The Tradewinds Series

# Promise Me Aloha

## Book five in the Tradewinds series

by
Taylor Bennett

Scriptures taken from the Holy Bible, New International Version®, NIV®. Copyright © 1973, 1978, 1984, 2011 by Biblica, Inc.™ Used by permission of Zondervan. All rights reserved worldwide. www.zondervan.com The "NIV" and "New International Version" are trademarks registered in the United States Patent and Trademark Office by Biblica, Inc.™

ISBN 978-1-953957-11-5
© 2021 Taylor Bennett

The Team: Miralee Ferrell, Alyssa Roat, Cindy Jackson
Cover Design: Indie Cover Design, Lynnette Bonner Designer

*Mountain Brook Ink is an inspirational publisher offering fiction you can believe in.*
Printed in the United States of America

# Acknowledgments

Each book that I write seems to be a little more of a challenge, which is why it isn't surprising that my tribe seems to grow with each new story that I tell. *Promise Me Aloha* was a labor of love—a story that was stuck deep in my heart and struggled to get out. I couldn't have released this story out in the world without my people, the incredible group of supporters that has never failed to cheer me on through every mountain and every valley of my writing journey.

First of all, Mom. Not only are you my lifelong proofreader and one of the few people brave enough to sit through a brainstorming session with me, but you're the person that keeps me sane. You're always there to walk with me, brew me a fresh mug of tea, and offer words of encouragement when I'm feeling stuck. Your constant belief in and support of me is overwhelming. Thank you for being the brightest spot, even on my cloudy days.

Dad, this one's for you. You might not be into "girl books," but you've never failed to cheer me on in your own special way. Thanks for not putting up too much of a fuss when I decide to beat you at cribbage whenever I need a brain break from drafting.

Miralee and Jenny—you are two of the best in the biz, the editors a writer could only dream of having. Your unending enthusiasm for my stories and the way you treat my characters like family is beyond special to me. I can't imagine where I (and Olive, Jazz, Brander, etc.) would be without your support and encouragement. You have made every one of my stories a thousand times better through your expert advice, and *Promise* is no exception.

Thanks also to Anna Schaffer, one of my very best writing buddies. You never fail to put a smile on my face (even from almost 3,000 miles away!) during one of our Skype calls. I love our conversations about everything bookish...and bread related. You're one of a kind!

Another shout out goes to my favorite trio of writers—the fabulous team behind GoTeenWriters.com. Stephanie, Shannon, and Jill, thanks for having my back from day one and cheering me on through every book launch since. If you're a young writer reading this right now, please know that there is no better writing resource on planet earth than their writing blog. The knowledge they have amassed on a single website over the past ten years is truly something to marvel at.

To my bookish friends and followers online—you're amazing!! Thank you for coming alongside me to love on and support my stories. Thank you for buying my books, for requesting them at your local library, and for loving Olive and the gang as much as I do. When I started writing, I dreamed of having a "fan base" and you have given me just that—a beautiful slice of the bookish community that I'm blessed to call my own. It's such a comfort to know that, as long as I keep writing, you'll keep reading.

Jesus—I wouldn't be writing these words right now if not for You. This is a story that I started out writing for me and ended up writing for *You*. From the first word to the first sentence to the first draft, You've had Your hand over *Promise Me Aloha* even before I have—and You've been writing my own love story just as carefully, too...

Elias LaLande, thank you—thank you for loving me, for stepping into my life at just the right moment, and for being the Brander to my Olive. I started writing this book with you as my "men's fashion guru" and I'm ending the journey with you as my fiancé. The Lord works in mysterious ways, and I couldn't be more excited to see where He leads us next.

# Dedication

*For Mom, who taught me the meaning*
*of aloha from the beginning*
and
*To Elias, I promise you my aloha...forever*

# Chapter One

SUNSET IS MY FAVORITE TIME OF DAY.

It's that time when the world unwinds. When the craziness of the day fades away and, even as darkness starts creeping in, the light somehow manages to prevail. When every day—good or bad—comes to an end and I get to look forward to starting over again in a few short hours.

But, unfortunately for me, sunset is still hours away.

Bright midafternoon sunlight glints off my rearview mirror as I pull into the driveway at Gramma's house, and I let the economy sedan's air conditioner blast on my face for a few more luxurious seconds before I shut off the ignition and race inside. It's barely even April, but the Hawaiian sun knows no seasons.

I let out a deep, long breath and grab a snack before settling onto the couch with my laptop to put the finishing touches on an article about the Great Banyan Tree's upcoming birthday party. In Maui, people will throw a luau for anything—even an ancient tree in the middle of town. And, unfortunately, when you're at the bottom of the food chain at the *West Maui Sun*, that's what you get stuck writing about.

I'd rather celebrate—or write about—something else, like the upcoming anniversary of when Brander and I officially started dating. But oh, well. Writing for the *West Maui Sun*, whether it's about bottlenose dolphins or banyan tree birthdays, is good for my bank account. Even if, on days like today, the work is absolutely mind-numbing.

If only I could escape to a deserted island somewhere and spend a few years learning how to be the next Jane Austen. That was always Mom's dream, and now, after spending four years at college studying English literature—some of the greatest stories on planet earth, it's mine too. If only Mom was still here, we could pool together our words to write...

"Aloha!" The front door bangs shut, snapping me out of my reverie before I can get *too* melancholy, and Jazz bounds into the living room, sporting a smile that's exceptionally wide—even for her. "Are you ready?"

"Ready for what?" I close my laptop and slide it onto the coffee table.

"Your *date*, duh. Brander told me you were going out tonight. I figured I'd come over and hang out with Macie." Ever since I moved here, Jazz's smile has shone brighter than the relentless Hawaiian sun, but today her grin is so big and warm that it's like she has a sudden urge to melt me into a puddle.

"What's with the theatrics? It's not like this is my first date."

"I know. But you *are* excited to see Brander. Right?"

"I'm always excited. Why wouldn't I be tonight?"

"No reason." Jazz gives a little jump, and her prosthetic leg clunks against the floor. She grimaces at the scratched-up metal pole attached to her left thigh, then shrugs and tugs at her Ho`opono `Ilio Rescue Center t-shirt. "I thought I'd come over and help you get dressed is all."

"What's wrong with what I'm wearing?" I glance at my work clothes. Crisply ironed white capris and a ruffled turquoise tank—way nicer than what Brander sees me wearing ninety-nine percent of the time.

"Nothing. But…"

"Fine. Style me." I throw up my hands in mock surrender. "Far be it from me to stand in your way." After all, Jazz has better design sense than anyone I know—even Brander's uber-rich mother, who keeps the Delacroix residence magazine-ready at all times.

"Yay!" Jazz practically skips over to the couch, and she pulls me up before I can even blink. "Come on—he'll be here in an hour."

I narrow my eyes at her as she proceeds to drag me upstairs. "How do *you* know that?"

Jazz's silvery eyes grow wide. "Uh, he and I were texting."

"About *my* date?"

"No…" Jazz's eyes widen into silver dollars. "About Hunter."

"Hunter, huh?" My lips twitch, and my tone turns just a slight bit cocky.

Brander's radar for talent shot way up the first time he heard Hunter play the drums during worship. After Brander graduated from college, they started a two-man worship band—Current. Thanks to a viral video that gave Brander five seconds of stardom back in high school, the two of them already have a loyal following. Yet, Hunter is still single.

And so is Jazz.

"Is our double wedding thing going to have a chance after all?" I make a show of crossing my fingers on both hands, and Jazz nearly stumbles over the landing steps when she gives me a swat.

"Don't get excited." She waves a finger in my face and hops up the last step before powering down the hallway. "I told you I'd never date anyone with a manbun, and I meant it. We weren't really talking about Hunter anyway. It's his sister, Breeze. She's on the autism spectrum. Hunter's parents have been worried about her since she started middle school. She's not adjusting as well as they'd hoped."

"They think a therapy dog would help?"

"That's the problem." Jazz slows to a stop outside the door to the bedroom I share with my little sister, Macie, then raises a hand and knocks. "They don't."

"But you do?"

"Doesn't *everyone* need a therapy dog?" Jazz puts both hands on her hips and lifts her chin.

"A therapy cat, maybe. But a dog? I don't know..." Macie's fluffy, scruffy shih tzu, Zuzu, yips from inside the room, as if proving my point.

"Yeah, yeah. That's just because you haven't met the right dog. One of these days you'll come around."

"Not a chance. Training therapy dogs is a noble profession and all, but I sure wouldn't want to be in your shoes."

Jazz wrinkles her nose. "I wouldn't exactly call picking up doggie doo *noble*."

"You know what I mean." I jerk my chin at the door, which has remained stubbornly shut this entire time. "Don't you think we should knock again?"

I bang on the door with a little more gusto and a lot less courtesy than Jazz did a minute before. "Macie?"

There's no answer other than Zuzu's squeaky little yip, but I take that as my cue to open the door anyway.

The fluffy mutt races out of the room like a furry rocket as Jazz and I step inside to find Macie slumped on her bed, poring over a magazine, headphones jammed over her ears. "Hey, Mace." I wave to get her attention, but she doesn't even twitch. I raise my voice. "Jazz is here."

Nothing.

"Macie!"

Nope.

I roll my eyes, march over to Macie's bed, and pluck a pair of sparkly pink earphones from her head of springy brown hair. "What has Grams told you about listening to your music too loud? You're going to need hearing aids just to finish seventh grade."

"What? I can't hear you."

"Very funny." I hand the headphones back to Macie, and she takes them, making a dramatic showing of lowering the volume before snapping them back on and turning another page in her magazine. "Seriously, Mace. Are you trying to go deaf?"

"Maybe. Then I wouldn't have to listen to you and Jazz talk about all your boring, grown-up problems all the time." Her voice is sour as a piece of Gramma's famous key lime pie, but her wink softens the blow. "Can't you guys hang out somewhere else? I'm busy."

"Reading a copy of *Baking Heaven*? That doesn't look too important to me." I lean over to get a peek at the magazine, the sight of a triple-decker chocolate cake making my mouth water. Dinner with Brander—or, more specifically, dessert—can't come soon enough.

"It is too important." Macie turns the page to an article on which types of flour result in the best crumb structure for a cake. "Grams and I need to try out a new recipe for—"

"Macie!" Jazz interjects so loudly I'll be surprised if *I'm* not deaf by the time Macie finishes seventh grade. "I think I hear Zuzu scratching at the front door."

"Downstairs?" Macie narrows her eyes at Jazz, as if try-ing to figure out how my friend suddenly developed supersonic hearing—which I myself am admittedly curious about. "How can you hear *that*?"

"Trust me. Go let her out, okay?"

Keeping one eye on Jazz, Macie abandons her magazine and earphones and backs out of the room. The second her footsteps fade, Jazz swings the door shut.

I'm about ready to ask Jazz why on earth everyone in this house is acting like their coconuts have cracked when she throws open my closet and sticks her head inside. "Ready to play fashion show? Come on—we don't have much time."

Like clockwork, by the time Brander parks his cherry-red Porsche in front of Gramma's house, Jazz has completely transformed my pathetic attempt at date-night attire into something...

"Wow." I sneak one last peek at myself in the mirrored closet door.

"You don't have to keep saying that." Jazz giggles from across the bedroom, where's she's peeping out the window at Brander.

"But it looks so *good*." I twist my sunrise shell neck-lace—the one Mom made for me so many years ago—around one hand as I smooth my yellow linen sundress with the other. It's not as dressy as what I'd had on before, but, with the ruffled hem and oversized bow in the back, it's a thou-sand times cuter. Paired with my favorite woven handbag and a pair of sea glass earrings, it's perfect. "How can you always make my clothes look so good when I can't?"

"Because, *ma cherie*. I have an eye for design." Jazz trills the last sentence in an ostensibly French accent. "Now come on. He's getting out of the car. And he has a *bouquet*."

"A bouquet, huh?" Brander's never brought flowers before. Malasadas, yes. Shave ice, for sure. But flowers? "I'm telling you, Jazz, there's something seriously weird going on today."

"Don't say that!" Jazz lunges toward me and grips my hand in her own as I head for the door. "It's supposed to be a good day."

"I didn't say it was *bad*. But you all are—"

The doorbell cuts me off, and Jazz nearly gallops down the stairs to answer it. I follow close behind. If Brander is acting anywhere near as weird as Jazz, I want a front-row seat.

"Hey." Brander pushes Koa wood sunglasses onto his head when Jazz opens the door, revealing wide, chocolate-colored eyes that hover above a pair of very pink cheeks. What was he doing after work today, sunbathing? It's not like he doesn't already have a tan—one that's accentuated by his blue-speckled white button-up.

"Hey." I meet him at the bottom of the stairs, and he gives me a hug punctuated with a quick kiss. "How was work?"

"Fine—the usual. How 'bout you?"

"Same."

"Good." His cheeks grow even pinker. Okay, so not sunburn—but why would he be blushing? It's not like going out on a Friday night is something new for either of us.

I shuffle my bare feet on Gramma's freshly swept floor. "Ready to go?"

He nods, his chin quivering so fast he looks like a bobblehead.

"Have fun, guys." Jazz offers a wave as I slip into the

shoes she picked out for me. "I'm going to go raid the fridge. Think *Tutu* Bonnie would mind?"

I laugh. "No way. Especially if you keep Macie out of trouble until Grams gets back from the gallery. Are you sure they won't miss you at the rescue?"

"Nah, I took the afternoon off. After all, it's a special—"

"Ready to go?" Brander asks again, louder this time. Before I can respond, he links his arm though mine, cupping his hand around my elbow and leading me out the front door into a world painted in promise by the golden rays of an almost-setting sun.

# Chapter Two

"Put this on." Brander hands me a square of fabric that looks sort of like a silky white kerchief as soon as we're buckled up in his car.

"Is that a..." I peer at the thing. "A bandana?"

"No, it's—never mind." He takes the piece of silk back. Before I ask what he's doing, he slips it over my eyes and knots it around my head.

"Hey! I can't see."

"That's the point." Brander gives my shoulder a quick squeeze before the Porsche roars to life, and we take off from the curb.

My stomach gives a lurch, though whether it's the usual burst of excitement over the evening ahead or a bit of queasiness from being blindfolded, I'm not quite sure. "This'd better not make me carsick."

"If driving the road to Hana doesn't make you carsick, nothing will. Hang tight, we'll be there soon."

"Where is *there*?"

"If I wanted you to know, I wouldn't have given you the blindfold."

"You're being awfully cryptic."

"I know."

"Jazz was acting weird too. You know anything about that?"

"Who, me?"

My heart gives a little flutter as we zip down the road

to—well, I wouldn't exactly know *where*, but something tells me whatever Brander has planned is going to be good.

Either that, or half the people on the island have finally cracked and I'm one of the few sane ones left. *Ha.* The voice in my head—the one that sounds a little bit like my mother—chuckles with me.

*Thanks a lot, Mom.*

"You know, this could be considered kidnapping," I say after a few moments of letting the breeze whip through my hair as we drive along to a soundtrack of croony old love songs.

"Except you didn't put up a fight."

"True." I lean against the buttery-smooth leather of the front seat, but before I can get too comfortable, Brander slows and puts the car in park. "Here already? What'd you do—drive around the block a few times?"

"Maybe." A car door opens and shuts, and then Brander's by my side, reaching for my hand and opening my own door. "Watch your step—it's kind of bumpy."

Thankfully Jazz was smart enough to outfit me in comfy woven sandals—unlike the mega-high-heeled shoes she picked out for my disaster of a first date a few years ago—so stumbling is no issue as Brander leads me along a slightly uneven concrete path.

On my left, ocean waves crash in my ear, and to the right, palm fronds rustle in the soft breeze. It's quiet, so we must not be strolling along the Ka'anapali Beach Walk. That means Front Street's out too. "Did we teleport somewhere or what?"

"Maybe." Brander tightens his hold on my hand.

"For real, where are we?"

"If I'm going to tell you that, then I might as well take off the blindfold." Brander releases me, and his hands come to rest on the nape of my neck.

"No, wait! I didn't...I mean—"

He laughs, the deep richness of his voice pooling in my ears like a silken ribbon of melted chocolate. "Don't worry. I was getting ready to anyway. Look."

The piece of silk drops away from my eyes, and I follow Brander's finger out to sea, where the sun is performing a precarious balancing act on the thin line of the horizon. Puffy clouds dance atop the skyline, first in front of, then behind the great orange fireball.

We *are* on the Ka'anapali Beach Walk after all—the non-touristy, city-owned part of it that encompasses a handful of oceanfront parks barely big enough for a few picnic tables each.

I lean into Brander's side, and he slips one arm around my shoulders, holding me tight. His bergamot cologne mingles with the almost-omnipresent aroma of plumeria to create a smell that, if bottled, would earn any perfume company millions of dollars in sales.

All too soon, the sun begins its descent beneath the waves, and Brander gives my hand a tug, leading me down the half-crumbling stairs to the beach. "Want to go for a walk?"

"Seeing as how you've taken me as your hostage, I guess I don't have a choice." I give him a light jab with my elbow. "Sure you don't want to 'fess up now?"

"Sure you don't want to wait and see for yourself?" He whispers in my ear, his breath tickling my cheek, then twines his fingers through my own as we meander along the deserted stretch of sand.

"It's quiet here tonight." Usually the Wahikuli Beach

Park is packed with people, whether it's a lazy Saturday afternoon or the middle of the day during the work week.

"Nice, isn't it?"

"Yeah." We stand for a minute, watching as the sun dives farther into the depths of the sparkling sea, but then something—a sign?—catches the corner of my eye.

I drop Brander's hand and walk closer to the old, weathered piece of plywood. The sign looks ancient, but I know I've never seen it here before. Without the help of the sun's brilliant rays, it's hard to make out the curling, spidery lettering on the board, but then a light shines on the board, illuminating the hand-lettered words.

*Reasons Why I Love You.*

"What is this?" I turn to Brander, who's aiming his phone's flashlight at the board, shuffling his feet, and patting his hair. He smiles, but it wavers a little—like he's seasick or something. Brander has never acted this nervous before—not even when he and Hunter gave their first concert last year.

"It's for you." He steps forward and bends to kiss my head—an easy feat, since that growth spurt I spent the better part of my teenage years waiting for never showed up. "I—I hope you like it." He leads me a few steps farther, to where another sign is stuck in the sand. This one is wrapped in a strand of twinkling lights.

Reason #1: *The way you smile when you think nobody's looking.*

"Hey!" I pretend to punch him in the arm. "What's wrong with the way I smile when people *are* looking?"

There's no time for him to answer though, because a wave breaks almost on my feet and washes over a large glass bottle, buried halfway in the sand in front of me. There's something inside. "Let me guess." I soften my smirk with a wink as I dig the bottle out of the sand and uncork it.

Inside is a list of reasons two through ten, including everything from the way I can't stop quoting Jane Austen to my obsession with coconut-flavored shave ice.

We keep wandering down the shore, occasionally stumbling across another sign or glass bottle. Along the way, strings of fairy lights and hanging lanterns guide our path. From somewhere far off in the distance, an acoustic version of "Time in a Bottle," one of Mom's favorite oldies—and therefore one of mine—serenades us.

"You didn't have to do all this, you know." I press a kiss to Brander's jaw in an attempt at a thank-you as the darkness around us deepens, wrapping me in a sweet cocoon of twilight and gratitude. "But I'm glad you did."

"Me too. Now come on. There's more to see."

He pulls me past several more signs until he stops at a picnic blanket in the sand. It's even darker out now, but half a dozen lanterns and strings of lights keep me from having to squint to read the last sign—Reason fifty.

*The way I know you'll stand by my side for the rest of my life...if you say yes.*

"What do you—" I turn to look at Brander but somehow, in the amount of time it took for me to read the sign, he's managed to drop to one knee and pick up a guitar.

The music that's been following us this whole time cuts out, and Brander starts to sing and play where the song left off. Except this time it means way more, because the words are coming straight from him to me.

Tears sting my eyes as he finishes and lays the guitar aside. Before I can thank him, Brander reaches down and lifts a pink-and-orange hued sunrise shell, the same kind as my necklace but way bigger. Something sparkles from within as he lifts it up to me.

"Brander—"

"Olive, would you—I mean, I really..." He dips his head and gives it a shake. "This was a lot easier when I was saying it to Jazz."

"Wait, what?"

"No, no, no." Brander shakes his head again, then shuffles his legs so he's kneeling on his other knee. "I mean I was practicing—"

"Maybe you'd better stand up for this."

"Maybe so." He scrambles to his feet, brushes sand from his knees, and clears his throat. "Olive, you are my very best friend. I can't imagine what life would be like without you. I—would you—"

"Let me get this straight." I take a step closer. The twinkle lights wrapped around a nearby palm tree sparkle in Brander's eyes. "Are you asking me to marry you?"

"Would you say yes if I did?"

My hug is the only answer either of us need. I wrap my arms around him and breathe in deep, but my breath catches in my throat when his lips meet mine.

Sure, Brander and I have kissed before, but this time— knowing that he's going to be the one that will hold me in his arms like this for the rest of my life...

*Wow.*

All of a sudden, a sizzling snap splits the air, and I jump, my heart pounding even faster than it was a moment ago. Brander takes my hand, and we stare at the sky as a silver-and-gold shower of sparks descends over the rippling black waters.

Then the darkness returns, and Brander pulls me back

into him. Once more, I'm enveloped in his embrace, half-smothered by his kiss in a way that makes my stomach twirl and my heart nearly ache. When he finally steps away, it's all too soon. Shadowed by the twilight, his face is nearly unreadable. I step closer. Lay one hand on his cheek. Feel the slight stubble beneath my fingertips.

"Is that a yes?" Brander's voice is low and husky, his eyes sparkling as if he's wishing upon a thousand stars. Dreaming about our future. *Together.*

I can barely recover my wits enough to speak—to give him the emphatic *yes* he deserves. Instead, I nod like a grinning idiot until my words return to me. "Of course. I mean, *yes.* I mean...I love you."

With that, Brander buries me in his embrace once more as sparks fill the darkness around us. A million voices fill the air, all shouting *Ho'omaika'i 'ana*—the Hawaiian way of saying congratulations.

And, as usual, one voice is louder than all the rest. "You're getting married!" Jazz's squeal rises above the melee of well-wishers, and she hands Gramma her still-fizzing sparkler before throwing herself at me and Brander. Hunter materializes and joins the group, squeezing us all into a group hug. Something tells me it's the first of many that we'll be experiencing tonight. Good thing my job benefits include health insurance, because Jazz and Hunter both look like they're out to break bones.

"Wait a minute." Brander pulls away and opens the shell box. "She doesn't even have her ring on yet."

"Yeah," I brush hair out of my face, and mock glare at Jazz. "And, to be honest, I don't quite know how to feel about all of this. After all, he proposed to you first."

"You *told* her about that?" Jazz's eyes go wide, and her gaze flashes more intensely than any sparkler. "What kind of a proposal was *that?*"

"A good one." I wrap an arm around Brander's waist. "He

got me to say yes."

"Don't you want to see your ring?" He reaches for my hand and slips something onto my ring finger. A perfect fit.

I lift my hand, and a white gold band studded with artfully arranged miniature diamonds—all of them winking up at a massive diamond in the middle—flashes in the light of a million sparklers.

"Congrats." A voice sneaks up on me from behind, and I whirl around to find Macie, brandishing an unlit sparkler in each hand. She hands one to me and the other to Brander, then Hunter procures a lighter and sends sparks flying.

A camera flashes somewhere, and conversation drifts down from further up the beach. Gramma waggles her fingers and blows me a kiss from where she's standing next to Brander's parents.

*Parents.*

A pang of sadness hits my chest—for Dad, all the way in Boston, who I'll have to wait to celebrate with later, and for Mom, who I'll never celebrate with again on this earth.

I blink hard once, twice, then refocus on Brander's parents.

August Delacroix has a huge grin on his pudgy pink face, but his wife Midori looks far more subdued. Not that that's much of a surprise. Even though Brander and I have known each other for years, his parents—correction, my future in-laws—are practically strangers.

"Come on, everyone." August claps his meaty hands and raises his voice over the excited din. "We have a party waiting for us at the resort, and the buffet tables are loaded."

There's nothing that can motivate the good people of Maui quite like the promise of food. The beach is deserted in less than a minute as everyone sets off down the Ka'anapali Beach Walk toward the Delacroixs' resort. Only Jazz and Hunter hang back with me and Brander, both of them gunning for attention.

"Good job, man." Hunter slaps Brander a high five.

"Are you proud of me, Olive? I've been keeping this a secret for *forever*." Jazz trots alongside me, her platinum-blonde braid bouncing. "You didn't guess, did you?"

"Never in a million years." I run my thumb over the band of the ring—the *engagement ring*—on my finger. The thrill and excitement of the evening buoys us along until we've caught up with the others at the open-air reception area of the Delacroix resort.

But we haven't even made it to the buffet table when Brander's mother sweeps in for a short, somewhat stiff hug. "Congratulations, my dear." She pulls away and brushes her tailored linen shift, as if she's afraid I could have sullied it with my own, much less glamorous, ensemble. "Come to brunch tomorrow and we'll discuss details for the wedding, yes?"

"Details? Who wants to think about details on a night like tonight?"

Mrs. Delacroix's eyes grow wide. "My dear, your wedding will be all *about* the details. If we don't start planning now—"

"Okay, okay." I hold up a hand to silence Mrs. Delacroix's rapid-fire stream of chatter. "Brunch sounds great."

After all, my dream wedding can't plan itself.

But for whatever reason, when I dreamed about me and Brander getting married, I forgot to write his parents into my perfect love story.

Especially his mother.

# Chapter Three

"YOU'RE SPENDING THE NIGHT." I GRAB Jazz's arm as the dinner party breaks up later that evening and pull her over to where Grams and Macie are making small talk with Mrs. Delacroix—or am I supposed to call Brander's mother by her first name now? "We have a *lot* to talk about. Think Dani would let you skip the night shift?"

"Actually, I can skip the whole *weekend*." Jazz beams her trademark Cheshire Cat grin. "Pre-planning pays off."

"Awesome."

Thanks to Dani and the Ho`opono `Ilio Rescue Center, Jazz gets her room and board —plus a small stipend of pay— in exchange for babysitting and training a pack of abandoned mutts every day and most nights too. Not the fairest of trades in my book, but I know that, for someone like Jazz, it's a dream come true.

"Did you like the cake tonight?" Macie crosses her arms over her stomach—not round like it was when she was little, but still soft enough to suggest that she spends a goodly amount of time sampling her own kitchen creations. "Grams and I spent all *day* on it while you were at work. It has a coconut-key lime compote in the middle."

"Does it?" My cheeks heat, and I duck my head. Brander and I were so busy getting hugged, congratulated, and posed for pictures that I didn't even know there *was* a cake.

"Yep. And coconut-vanilla buttercream. But of course, you'd know that...if you'd eaten any of it." She hangs her head, and a ribbon of guilt threads through my otherwise-empty stomach.

"Mace, I'm sorry. I'd love to try a piece of your cake. In fact—" Before I can finish that thought, my stomach cuts me off with an audible groan mighty enough to replace Macie's frown with a cocky grin.

She rolls her eyes. "Good thing there's some left over. We can finish it off at home."

"Olive?" Brander walks over to us, his leather boat shoes squeaking against the polished teak floor of the open-air banquet room. "Did my mom talk to you?"

"About tomorrow?"

"Yeah. Can you come around eleven?"

"Sure." My eyes dart over Jazz, then Macie, and finally Gramma before resting on Brander. "Can I bring everyone else?"

"I was hoping you would." His almond-shaped eyes crinkle around the edges. "See you tomorrow."

"See you then." I step over to give him one more hug—the last of many tonight—and he brushes a soft kiss over my lips. One that I deepen—just for a moment.

"I love you." We say it at the same time and laugh as we pull apart and go our separate ways.

"I can't wait for tomorrow," I say over my shoulder, the words coming out almost shyly as I stare across the room, illuminated by a thousand twinkle lights, at Brander. *My fiancé.* "But I'd better head out. It sounds like I have a cake to eat."

"You know what?" Jazz slings one arm around me and the other around Macie as we make our way back to the Ka'anapali Beach Walk. "I think those might be the best words I've heard all day. 'Course, I'm not the one who got proposed to tonight."

"Don't worry." I give her a side-eyed smirk. "It sounds like you've been proposed to quite enough lately."

The next morning, a very flour-covered version of Abigail Kaye, the Delacroix housekeeper, opens the double doors leading to the Delacroix mansion with a squeal that makes her sound like a giddy teenager.

"Congratulations, Olive!" She beams extra-wide at me, her eyelids crinkling like layers of flaky puff pastry behind her tortoiseshell glasses. "I'm so happy for you. Brander told me about his surprise ages ago, and I've been helping Midori plan this brunch ever since. Come in, come in. I made a cake!"

At the thought of *more* cake, I can't help but smile even wider than I already am. In other words, my face seriously feels like it's going to split in two. No matter. There's Brander for me to hug, cake for me to eat—not to mention a whole bunch of other, sure-to-be-delicious food too. After all, Abigail and Grams were cut from the same cloth—only, Gramma happens to come in extra-large.

Too bad Brander's mom isn't more like Abigail. I've only met the bubbly Delacroix housekeeper a handful of times, but even so, she's a thousand times easier to be around than Mrs. Delacroix.

Speaking of whom...

"You brought your entourage, I see." She sweeps around a corner, wearing a sky-blue sheath dress that looks more appropriate for a business meeting than a celebratory brunch. "Brander said you might."

"Where is Brander, anyway?" I peer behind her into the

two-story open-air living room, where a dining table over-looking the ocean has been set for seven.

"He'll be along." Mrs. Delacroix waves a hand. "He and August are in the middle of a conference call."

"At eleven o'clock?"

I pop the question as Jazz squeaks. "On a Saturday?"

Mrs. Delacroix stares at us as if we're both nuts. "The resort doesn't close for the weekend. A business executive's work is never over. I hope you're aware of that, Olivia."

I bite my lip. Now is probably not the time to mention that, for one, my name is *Olive.* And, for two, if being a business executive means spending the morning working—on a *Saturday*—the day after you get engaged, I'm not quite sure Brander's cut out to be one.

Thankfully, before I lose my last ounce of self-control and spit the words out anyway, Brander and his beaming, bald, bowling-ball of a dad round the corner, both sharply dressed in white-collared linen shirts.

Good thing Jazz convinced me to wear a skirt.

"Hey, guys." Brander gives Jazz and Macie fist bumps, then swoops in to hug Grams before wrapping his arms around me and squeezing tight. There may or may not also be a kiss involved too. "Ready to eat?"

"I'm *starving.*" Macie eyes Abigail's flour-dusted apron approvingly. "Do I smell biscuits?"

"You have a good nose." Abigail motions to the Delacroixs' massive kitchen island, which has been transformed into a buffet table of sorts. "Help yourselves."

We do and, in a matter of minutes, everyone is seated at the table. Lucky me, I'm sitting right next to Mrs. Delacroix. Brander's dad offers Brander and me his congratulations again—followed by a nice, albeit slightly stiff, blessing for the food before we dig in.

My mouth is stuffed full of honey-buttered biscuit and candied bacon when Mrs. Delacroix taps one long, French-manicured fingernail against her fluted glass of tomato juice.

"Shall we begin?" She pushes aside a half-eaten plate of egg white frittata and reaches for a small notebook by her elbow. "Abi, could you hand me a pen?"

The Delacroix housekeeper materializes—almost out of thin air—and pulls a fountain pen from her pocket. Midori snatches the pen out of Abigail's open hand without a word, uncaps it, and scribbles something in her notebook. "I know how busy we all are." She peers at everyone gathered around the table, as if the fact that we all have full, vibrant lives is some sort of a problem. "This is the perfect opportunity for us to discuss the details of this affair."

*Details? We haven't even been engaged for twenty-four hours, and you expect us to be ready to talk about details?*

Thank goodness for the biscuit on my plate. I take an extra-big bite, close my mouth, and chew to keep the half-dozen snarky responses whirling around in my brain from popping out. By the time I finish chewing, hopefully Brander will have come up with an appropriately polite answer.

I chew as long as I can, but there's no such luck. In fact, if I didn't know any better, I'd think Brander was trying out my own evasion strategy.

*Oh, fine.*

I swallow hard, then open my mouth. "What kind of de-tails, exactly?"

"Oh. You know." Midori swats a hand in the air, as if that should be answer enough. "Wedding date, venue, number of guests. Perhaps where you'd like to register. The basics."

I bite my lip. "We haven't—I mean, Brander and I haven't had much time to talk about that kind of stuff."

Mrs. Delacroix taps her fountain pen against the notebook, as if she's already growing impatient. "What about next June, then?"

"*Next June?*" I almost catapult from my seat, and I probably would if not for the sudden presence of Brander's hand on my knee.

"Okaasan." His voice is quiet, almost reverent, as if he's afraid of angering his mother. "That's over a year away."

"Exactly." Mrs. Delacroix smooths her slick mane of ebony hair. "It'll give us plenty of time to make arrangements. You certainly can't expect to have a June wedding this year. There's no time. Besides, the resort is booked out through August."

"Who said anything about June? And why do we need time, anyway?" The words erupt from my mouth in a way that sends Midori's lips pursing into a prickly frown. I take a deep breath that will hopefully soften my tone before going on. "I don't want a big, fancy resort ceremony. I want to get married on the beach."

"That sounds perfect." Brander squeezes my knee beneath the table. "Like the perfect fit for *us*."

"But—but..." Brander's mother sputters like a dying boat engine. "That's..."

"Perfect," Jazz clasps her hands. "I mean, Olive and Bander practically met on the beach. They got engaged on the beach. Is there any other place for them *to* get married?"

"But the resort..." Mrs. Delacroix sighs weakly. "Auggie?"

I almost choke on my last bite of biscuit at Mrs.

Delacroix's pet name for her husband. Brander pats my back and I cough into my napkin while Mr. Delacroix chimes in. "What Midori is saying is that the resort is fully equipped to help you two have the wedding of your dreams. But all of our event spaces are already booked through the summer. Waiting until next year will allow you two to plan every detail, even the brand of soap in the bathrooms."

He has *got* to be kidding.

"In fact, if you pick the scent you'd like today, I can get in touch with my supplier and arrange a shipment for next May."

He's not kidding.

"Listen, Mr. Delacroix—"

"Call me August. Or Auggie. Either works." He holds up a big, meaty hand and beams a toothy grin. "After all, you're part of the family now."

*Part of the family.* The words make the biscuit in my stomach turn over in giddy little somersaults, but not even the thought of sharing Brander's last name can keep me from the task at hand. "Okay, August. I appreciate you wanting to help with the wedding and stuff, but you don't need to. My dad always said—"

"I know we don't *need* to, but we *want* to, dear." Mrs. Delacroix—oops, I guess that would be Midori now—lays a small, cold hand on my arm.

"Well...um..." I drop my head. "Brander?"

Brander reaches across the table to lay a hand on Midori's arm. "Mom, we don't need a big, elaborate wedding. And if it means waiting an entire year—"

"*Over* a year."

"Right. We don't want to wait that long. We'd rather a nice, simple ceremony in...I don't know. When do you want to get married, Olive?"

"I guess I haven't really thought about it, but why wait?"

"Because..." Mrs. Delacroix purses her lips. I can practically see the entire planning session slipping through her hands like yards and yards of the white silk she probably wants me to wear as I walk down the aisle. Which, by the way, is *not* happening. "There are *still* arrangements to be made—and the reception. You can't have *that* on the beach."

"Fine." I cross my arms and slouch in my chair until Jazz catches my eye from across the table. She waggles her finger in my direction and flashes an overeager grin, as if telling me to shape up.

Which I should.

Before I can attempt to smooth things over, Gramma comes to my rescue with a soft clear of her throat. "Midori, surely you must remember what it's like to be young and in love. It's not fair to expect them to wait so long. Maybe we can compromise. What's the shortest amount of time you'd need to plan this grand event?"

"Auggie?" Midori taps one finger against her chin, cocking her head at her husband across the table.

"I don't see why we couldn't pull things together by September. I have friends in high places, you know."

Midori opens her mouth, as if to object, but August continues. "The whole hotel staff loves Brander. If making his big day special means putting in a bit of extra elbow grease, they'll do it."

"Fine," Midori sounds a little like Macie does when she's in a mood. Brander's mother must be beyond slumping in her chair though, because her posture only seems to grow stiffer. "A September wedding. That could be worse. Though I don't know where you'll go for your honeymoon. August and I married in the fall, and our trip to Venice was nearly canceled due to flooding."

"We can worry about that later, Okaasan." Brander grips my hand under the table. "Olive, what do you think? Is September our answer?"

"Sure." If it was up to me, I would've picked June—*this* June. The same month Mom and Dad got married. But, much as I hate to admit it, I kind of get Mrs. Delacroix's point. There's still one thing, though. "Um, August. Midori."

Their eyes lock on me, and I swallow.

"I appreciate that you want to have the wedding at your resort, and I think it would be cool and everything, but..." Pinpricks of heat dance up my cheeks. How can I help them understand that I don't *want* a resort-style wedding with towering balloon arches and a five-course reception dinner?

That, in this moment, all I want is *love*.

"Please, dear." Midori's hand brushes my own. "Don't worry about the finances. August and I completely understand that your family comes from a different socioeconomic status. We'd be more than happy to—"

"Whoa, Mom." Brander's eyes fly wide open, growing so large and round that they practically eclipse his face. And here I thought that kind of thing only happened in cartoons. "Let Olive finish. You don't even know that's what she was going to say."

Mrs. Delacroix's entire face turns almost as red as the tomatoes studding her uneaten frittata. "Oh. Well. Go ahead."

"Actually, Mrs. Delacroix, you raise a good point. My family *is* too poor to book out your resort. And, much as I appreciate the help—"

"There's no need to be shy. Like Auggie said, we're all

family now."

"Ah-*hem*." Jazz clears her throat from across the table, where she, Grams, and Macie have been sitting like three lumps of volcanic rock. "I think what Olive's trying to say is that she doesn't *want* a big, fancy resort ceremony. She wants something simpler, more intimate. You know?"

"No." Mrs. Delacroix sticks her nose in the air. "I absolutely do *not* know. The resort's venue is straight out of a fairytale. Who wouldn't want to take advantage of it?"

"Okay, time *out*." Macie pushes away from the table and throws her fancy cloth napkin onto her plate of half-finished biscuits and gravy. "Olive didn't even know she was getting married until yesterday. I thought we were here for a celebration, not an interrogation." She finishes with a huff and collapses into her chair. A smirk plumps her freckled cheeks, like she thinks she's doing me a favor by insulting our host.

Which, maybe she is, if the sheepish half-smile spreading across Midori's face is anything to go by. "I suppose you have a point." Without another word, Brander's mom caps her pen and pushes it and her notepad aside before taking a bite of what must now be ice-cold frittata. Jazz and Gramma shoot Macie looks riddled with thanks, and I offer a quick thumbs-up from my spot across the table.

Macie offers a smug smile in return, inclining her head like the triumph has made her honorary royalty, but then she hunches her shoulders and leans both elbows on the table, apparently too exasperated to even lift her fork.

It's all enough to make me wonder...

Would anybody mind if Brander and I decided to elope?

# Chapter Four

"GUESS WHAT." SOMEONE SNEAKS UP BEHIND me and whispers in my ear before church starts Sunday morning, their softly spoken words tickling my neck.

"Geesh, you shouldn't sneak up on people like that." I turn around and pretend to swat at Brander, who's standing one row back. "What's up?"

"Guess."

"Your mom decided we need to have a destination wedding in Fiji?"

"Because Hawaii isn't exotic enough?" Jazz must've overheard at least part of our exchange, because she walks up with a smile on her face.

"Whoa, hold on." Brander reaches up to run a hand through his out-of-control hair. "Enough guessing, okay? This doesn't have anything to do with my mom."

*Thank goodness.* "Then what's it about?"

"Lunch."

"Ooh. I love lunch." Jazz licks her lips, then glances between me and Brander. "But something tells me I'm probably not invited."

"Not this time." Brander runs a hand over his cowlick. "I asked Jonah if he'd do our premarital counseling, and he'd like to meet for lunch today to get things started."

"You mean like today-today?" Jazz's eyes grow wide. "You've only been engaged for two days. What about the honeymoon phase and all that?"

"The honeymoon phase is supposed to come *after* you get married." I poke her in the ribs. "But it *is* awfully soon, isn't it?" Even as I say the words, something funny flickers in my stomach. Why does premarital counseling have to sound so...*serious?*

I bite my lip. Why can't Brander and I get lunch together—like, the two of us? The time he and I get to spend alone seems to have been condensed into a few precious seconds ever since he slipped this diamond-encrusted ring onto my finger.

Then again, if Jonah has any advice for dealing with future in-laws, then it might be a worthwhile endeavor. "Fine. It's a go."

Brander's eyes light up. "Awesome! Where do you want to eat?"

"Do you even have to ask?"

"Fleetwood's it is." Brander offers a double thumbs-up then dashes off.

"Premarital counseling, huh?" Jazz raises a hand, as if to wipe a tear from her eye. "My best friend is all grown up."

"Wait till it's your turn." I point with my elbow to where Hunter is hovering near the stage, staring at us—or, more likely, Jazz. "Maybe you should go talk to Hunter about getting that dog for his sister."

Jazz's cheeks turn a brilliant shade of flamingo pink, and she ducks to adjust her prosthesis liner. "*Stop.* It's not my fault he's suddenly obsessed with therapy dogs."

"*Sure.* Since when is dealing with potential customers part of your job description? I thought you were all about the mutts."

Unfortunately, before Jazz can answer, my matchmaking efforts fly into the bay as Hunter steps onstage to join

Brander in kicking off the worship set. As the first few chords and drum beats ring out over the packed pavilion, a little thrill zips through my heart.

Here I am, on the island that I love, with the people that I love, worshiping the God that I love. That might sound cheesy, but I don't care. It's *true*, and it's one of the best feelings in the world.

Here's hoping I can channel this kind of mountaintop-style peace and joy when Jonah starts grilling me and Brander about our five-year plan for the future.

Or whatever else premarital counseling includes.

A few hours later, Brander, Jonah, and I are huddled around a table on Fleetwood's famous rooftop deck overlooking the Lahaina harbor. A handful of surfers keep the scene lively, their boards carving great arcs through the foamy water beyond the breakwall.

"What's good here?" Jonah runs his hand over the scruffy goatee he started growing last summer—to make him look more assertive now that he's in his thirties, he says—and peers at the menu.

"What do you suggest, Olive?" Brander nudges me. "Since you've had everything on the menu *at least* ten times."

"He's right." Ever since Brander brought me here for lunch the first year I lived in Hawaii—when we were "just friends"—I've been hooked on the restaurant's killer food and classic rock-n-roll vibe. Even when Brander was at college in Honolulu, we always ended up here as many times as possible during his visits home. And no matter how many times I sit on this rooftop, I can't help but think the same thing—*Mom would've loved it here.* "I usually end up with the shrimp-and-lobster roll, but you can't go wrong with anything—especially with the Lahaina Burger."

"Okay then." Jonah lays his menu on the table. "Burger it is."

The waiter comes around soon after that to take our orders, then Jonah steeples his fingers and opens his mouth.

But, before he can say a word, my phone pings with a text. I fumble in my pocket to silence it, sneaking a peek at the screen as I do. It's from Mrs. Delacroix—er, Midori. Probably trying to get me to reconsider that eighteen-months-away wedding date. *No, thank you.*

"Are you ready?" Brander nudges my foot under the table.

"Yeah. Sorry." I shove the phone in my pocket and focus on Jonah. "It's on silent now."

"Great." Jonah claps his hands together and leans forward, then gives us the scoop on everything we'll need to know about the impending "exploration of our ever-deepening relationship with each other and the Lord." Which to be honest, sounds even more intimidating than what I was expecting. I mean, I thought I'd kissed homework goodbye when I graduated college. Now I have a massive workbook that's nearly the size of my junior-year literature textbook.

By the time lunch arrives, we're not even halfway through the first chapter's list of talking points, and my mouth is drier than a piece of sunbaked cardboard. Brander must pick up on my nerves, because he gives my hand an extra-tight squeeze as we bow our heads to pray.

When we finish, Jonah cocks his head at me. "What's on your mind, Olive?"

I take a drink of water to loosen my tongue, but it barely

helps. "This is all a little much, don't you think? Work, wedding planning—now homework too?"

"Whoa, wait up." Brander reaches over to steal one of my extra-crispy fries. "You're not alone in this. You have God, you have Jonah, and you have *me*."

"Thank goodness." I snag a golden-brown fry from his plate so we're even.

"And you know my mom means well, right?" Brander swats my hand away from his plate before I can snatch another fry. "I'm sure that once the excitement has worn off, she'll calm down some. She might not be good at showing it, but she honestly does want the best for you—for us."

"In-law trouble already?" Jonah peers at me around his massive burger, his eyes dancing. If I didn't know better, I'd think he was trying hard not to laugh.

Then again, he *does* know Midori Delacroix.

And, since Jonah knows Midori, maybe that means there's a chance he can help make sure that she doesn't turn my dream wedding into a million-dollar nightmare.

"Olive!" Dad's voice practically squeaks out my name, making him sound more like a middle-schooler than a college professor when I call him later that night. "How are you?"

"I'm good, Dad. How are you?"

"Good? Shouldn't you be wonderful? Amazing? Fantastic? You're engaged to the love of your life. What's wrong?"

"Nothing. Why would you think that there was?"

"Olive, I'm your father."

"Yeah... "

"And a psychology professor."

"Fair point."

"In that case, then, what on the valley isle could possibly be wrong? Other than the fact that you waited until two days after your engagement to finally call your beloved father and tell him the good news in person, that is."

"Sorry." I lean against the cushion that Macie and I finally convinced Grams to buy for the old, splintery porch swing. "Jazz came over to spend the night on Friday, and then yesterday—"

"Never you mind, that was all in jest. After all, there are far more interesting men in your life nowadays than your dear old dad. But still the question remains. What's wrong?"

"Nothing." I blow out a breath of air and stare past the crashing ocean waves to the brilliant late-afternoon sky. "Nothing...except for this whole wedding thing."

"Cold feet, already? Don't be alarmed. You know your mother almost called off our wedding at the rehearsal dinner."

While every bit of my heart yearns to listen to Dad tell old stories about him and Mom, another part of me knows that getting all teary-eyed and nostalgic won't be any help right now. "I'm not worried about getting married—it's the *wedding*. My dream wedding is a little different than what Brander's mom has in mind."

"Ah. In-laws." Dad falls silent. "That, I'm afraid, will take more than an amusing anecdote to fix."

"What about a dad's point of view?"

"That could be arranged."

I tell him everything about yesterday's brunch and the subsequent twenty-five texts—I counted—from Mrs. Delacroix, each one proposing a completely different and totally over-the-top idea.

Wedding dresses with twelve-foot trains? A glass dance

floor with an aquarium underneath? A photo booth made out of a life-sized copy of *Pride and Prejudice*?

Yes, yes, and yes—or, in my humble opinion, *no, no, no.*

But Dad simply chuckles as I rattle off the list. "Olive, you've hit the jackpot. You'll have the wedding of the century."

"Come on, Dad." I snort. "This is *my* wedding we're talking about, and I think it's ridiculous. It's like—like saying that everyone needs to have a twenty-four-karat gold tassel on their cap and a silver-plated zipper on their gown just to graduate"

Dad sputters with laughter. "Olive, for heaven's sake. This is your *wedding.* Don't you want it to be like something from a fairy tale?"

I can't help but agree with him on that, but at the same time...

What if my fairy tale isn't everyone else's Cinderella story?

"Then tell her how you feel," Jazz says on the phone later that night, a chorus of dog yips and barks backing her words. "What's the worst that could happen?"

"She'll think I'm turning into a massive bridezilla."

"Are you?"

I rest my head in my free hand. "I don't know."

"That's a yes." Another yip punctuates Jazz's short pause. "What are you doing after work tomorrow?"

"Nothing. Why?"

"You're coming over. There's no better cure for being a bridezilla than getting covered in doggie slobber."

"For real?" I groan. Four years of living in the same

house as Macie's mangy—though admittedly cute—mutt still haven't completely cured me of my dog phobia. Especially when it comes to big dogs, like the Delacroixs' infamous guard dog, Rosco. Speaking of which... "Oh, no. Jazz!"

"What?" She mimics my panicked tone, then coughs, as if trying to smother a giggle. "Did Mrs. Delacroix text you again?" This time she *does* laugh.

"No, this is serious. What if Brander wants to bring Rosco with him when he moves out?" I shudder at the thought of Rosco—a ninety-pound German Shepherd made of solid muscle and very few brain cells—snuggled between me and Brander in bed every night.

*Nope. Nada. Never gonna happen.*

"Olive. Are you still there?" Jazz's question is nearly lost beneath the howl of a dog. Footsteps slap against the floor, and Jazz mutters something under her breath.

"Yeah, I'm there. Are the dogs okay?"

She harrumphs, and a door bangs shut on her end. "Fine. Just a Chihuahua with major adjustment issues. Mijo hasn't slept through the night once since he got dropped off."

"That's why I'm never having kids," I grumble as the howls on Jazz's end get louder. "It's a wonder you guys still have any neighbors."

"Whoa, wait a minute." Something slams and the howls turn to quiet yips, then fade away altogether. "You don't want to have kids?"

"I'd make an awful excuse for a mom. Why?"

"Well, maybe...I mean, Brander's kind of a family guy. Is he up for that?"

"Oh." I bite my lip. "I guess—I mean, we haven't talked about it much."

"Geesh, if you didn't talk about that then what *did* you and Jonah talk about today? Aren't pets and house rules and kids what premarital counseling is all about?"

I open my mouth to respond, but Jazz interrupts me with a shriek.

"You okay?"

"Dani didn't tell me this guy was a piddler."

"Ew." I wrinkle my nose. "You'd better make sure he's locked up when I come over tomorrow."

"No problem. When do you get off work?"

"Four. You're sure that mongrel will be out of my hair?"

"Consider it done."

I cross my fingers. "I'm counting on it."

# Chapter Five

"Mijo! Mijo!" Jazz runs out of the ramshackle-house-turned-doggie-rescue-mission and into the chain-link-fenced front yard, flailing her arms like she's a windmill. She keeps her eyes fixed on a galloping whiteish blur, barely looking up until the mutt stops to investigate a pile of doggie poo nearly as big as he is. "Olive!" Her arms start waving even faster. "Don't open that gate or he'll get out."

"Is that the piddler?" I take a step back, even though I'm only halfway across the sidewalk.

"One and the same." Jazz pushes an escaped strand of hair into her braid and sneaks over to where Mijo is loitering, his scruffy legs half-buried in the unmowed lawn. "He's been playing keep-away all afternoon."

"Where's Dani? Can't she help?"

"I wish. She's in Kahului, looking into a possible puppy mill situation."

Right then, someone clears their throat behind me. "Um, is this a bad time?"

"A bad time for what?" I turn to find Hunter, his dirt-blond hair scraped into a low ponytail, overgrown stubble shading his jaw. "I thought Brander said you guys had band practice today."

"Not until five. I was in the neighborhood, so I thought I'd drop by." His response is directed at me, but his gaze keeps sneaking over to Jazz. "But if you guys are busy..."

"No, no. Come on in." In one swift swoop, Jazz picks up

the hairiest, ugliest chihuahua I've ever seen and nestles him in the crook of her arm. "This little guy won't be going anywhere for a very long time. Isn't that right, Mijo?"

As if in answer, the dog gets a nasty little gleam in his eyes, and something soaks through the front of Jazz's shirt, turning it sopping wet. "Eww, Mijo!" Without looking either of us in the eye, Jazz edges toward the front door. "Give me a minute, okay?"

"As many as you need." Hunter's tone is even, but there's a strange half-smile on his face as he follows Jazz inside with his eyes. "She realizes there are plenty of good jobs out there that *wouldn't* result in her getting covered in dog pee, right?" He asks once Jazz is safely out of earshot.

"She'd never leave this place." I unlock the gate, lead Hunter up the front path to a small porch, and motion for him to take a seat on a metal camp chair. "Her heart's too involved. She loves giving animals a second chance."

"I guess." Hunter shrugs. "I'd rather deal with an angry customer than an angry pit bull."

"You and me both. How are things at the Shave Ice Shack?" Between helping with the youth ministry at church and managing the band's social media accounts, Hunter barely has time to hold down a part-time position at the Shave Ice Shack, but somehow he manages.

"Crazy. There was an hour-long wait last Saturday."

"An hour? Sheesh." I cringe at the thought. Working my way through college in that cramped breadbox of a snack shack taught me that it takes a certain breed to put up with the                                                          job. "Guess Kaanapali Beach's favorite hidden gem isn't so hidden anymore?"

"The mainlanders have taken over. I miss dealing with

the kamaʻāina—the locals. I'd like to start giving out free af-ter-school kiddie cones or something. Remind the regulars that we aren't just a tourist operation."

"No way you'd get the owner to go for that." I shake my head. The thought of the Shave Ice Shack's burly, tattooed owner going so far as to give out free shave ice is laughable. "He's a beast."

"Hank? A beast? Nah. He's an old softie when you get to know him. Especially now."

I'm about to ask what he means by *now*, but Jazz appears before I can. She's sporting the same fraying pair of shorts, a fresh t-shirt, and a sheepish smile. "Sorry about that. Hunter, next time you want to talk dog business, make an appointment, okay?"

"I could come tomorrow if this isn't—"

"I was kidding, silly." Jazz rolls her eyes, but she's smil-ing too. "Consider that a warning, though—some of our new arrivals aren't exactly toilet trained."

"You don't say." I snort. "So Hunter, your sister likes dogs?"

"Breeze, uh...she doesn't—"

"She doesn't talk a lot, does she?" Jazz's eyes are wide and sympathetic.

"No. But she loves stuffed animals. I thought maybe..."

"Absolutely." Jazz spins on her heel, her braid swishing behind her, and motions for us to follow suit. "Let's go into the office and I'll get you lined up with some paperwork, okay?"

A few minutes and another ink cartridge later, Hunter is heading out the door with a stack of freshly printed pa-perwork almost as thick as the extra-thick tourist edition of the *West Maui Sun* I had the displeasure of proofreading today.

"You're good at this." I give Jazz a look as we head down the hall to her "office"—aka her bedroom. "I bet Hunter thinks so too."

Jazz lifts her chin and ushers me into her room, as if pointedly ignoring my comment. "We're supposed to be talking about you, not me. And definitely not about Hunter."

I snap my fingers, as if in defeat. "I tried."

"Seriously though." Jazz reaches into her mini fridge for a can of the passionfruit juice that runs through the veins of half of Hawaii's population before collapsing onto her bed. "For someone who's engaged to the love of their life, you sure don't seem very excited about it. What gives?" "Wait a minute. Of course I'm excited about being engaged."

"You sure aren't acting like it."

The words hit me in the gut like a sneaker wave. I flop next to Jazz on the worn, hibiscus-print quilt and twist my ring around and around my finger. The tiny diamonds on the vintage-style milgrain band flash in the late-afternoon sunlight streaming in between Jazz's blinds. One thought of standing in the sand, looking into Brander's chocolate-colored eyes, and promising myself to him forever is enough to make me want to dance all the way to the chapel of love. So... "Sure, I'm excited. It's my dream come true."

"Have you told that to your face lately?" Jazz quirks an eyebrow in my direction and takes a long slurp from her can as I keep twisting the ring, the giant diamond in the center glinting up at me.

"Brander must've spent a fortune on this thing."

"What does that have to do with anything?"

"Nothing. It's perfect—*he's* perfect."

"Okaaay..." Jazz cocks her head at me.

"He's perfect, but we've barely even seen each other since we got engaged. And when we do, we're doing premarital counseling or wedding planning or...*work*."

"Then don't." Jazz says it so simply that she makes me sound like a fool. "Go over to his house right now and invite him to go out to dinner—the two of you. Forget about wedding planning and counseling and go have *fun*."

"But he and Hunter have band practice."

"Crash it."

"I can't get all clingy now—just because I have a ring on my finger."

"Come *on*." Jazz sits up straight, like someone slipped a steel rod down her shirt, and nudges my arm. "You're not being clingy, you're being rational. Now go home, put some powder on your nose, and go crash that band practice."

I ring the doorbell once.

Twice.

Three times and the drum beat spilling from the open windows of the Delacroixs' guest-house-turned-bachelor-pad still overpowers the bell's insistent chiming.

*Okay, you asked for it.*

Hands on my hips, I march around the side of the house and step close to wave through the glass sliding back door. Brander's head is bowed low over his guitar, his hair flip-flopping in time with the tempo, but Hunter must see me because the drums stop mid-beat. Brander lifts his head and waves, then hurries to open the door. "Olive?"

"Hey. I um, I mean..." *Here's the deal—I thought I'd crash your rehearsal so I could tell you how much I've missed you, even though we've seen each other every day since we got engaged.* I duck my head, a sudden swirl of emotions wrapping around my heart.

Have I even gotten a chance to tell Brander how much I love him since he asked me to be his wife?

My eye itches. I lift a hand to scratch it and, when I bring it down, there's a telltale streak of black on my finger. *No, no, no.* I keep my head low and mumble something about him needing to get back to work.

"Olive, are you okay?" Brander steps barefoot onto the patio and puts a hand on either side of my face, lifting it to meet his own. "What happened?"

"Nothing. I mean, Jazz said—I knew this was a bad idea."

"Hunter?" Brander leans over to yell into the house. "Let's wrap it up for today."

"Copy that." Hunter's voice is loud and booming, as though he's conveniently oblivious to the relationship drama happening right out back. "See ya Wednesday." The front door slams a few seconds later.

"Let's try this again." Brander pulls me closer and gives me a hug, punctuated with a quick kiss. "Now, what's up?"

It's right on the tip of my tongue to tell him everything—how much stress this wedding business has suddenly piled onto my plate, how little time we're actually getting to spend together, the works—but suddenly the only words that seem right are short and sweet. "Want to get a shave ice?"

"Something tells me there's more on your mind than shave ice. Can you tell me what's wrong first?"

"It's the wedding." The words burst out before I can stop them, and Brander's usually golden skin fades to coconut white. If I wasn't still wearing my fancy, strappy work shoes, I would totally be sticking my foot in my mouth right now.

"Maybe we'd better sit." Brander plops onto the concrete steps leading from his cottage to the patio and puts his head in his hands.

"Wait." I settle onto the step next to him. "I don't mean I'm stressed about *marrying* you. But the whole planning business is freaking me out. Besides that, ever since we got engaged, we've barely had a chance to actually—you know—*be engaged.*"

A smile illuminates Brander's face like sunlight breaking through clouds after an afternoon squall. "I was just telling Hunter the same thing. I've missed you—even if we have been together every day."

"I've missed you too." I lean into him. "But what are we going to do? I mean, we both have jobs, and this wedding isn't going to plan itself."

"We'll make it work." Brander nudges my arm. "I promise."

"How? I'm starting to think it'd be easier to elope."

Brander coughs into the palm of his hand, but to my ears it sounds more like a laugh. "My mom would flip."

I trace my finger along the band of my ring. "Would you?"

"No." He shakes his head. "All I want is for you to be happy. Would you be happy if we eloped?"

I snort. "Hardly. I want to get married in front of all my *ohana.* I want to pay an arm and a leg to get a bunch of pictures taken of us so we can put them in an album and get all misty-eyed over them when we're fifty. I want to cut up a fancy cake and shove it in your face—no offense."

"None taken." One corner of Brander's mouth turns up. "What else?"

For the first time since Brander slid this ring on my

finger, I close my eyes and drift away on a sea of memories and dreams—memories of childhood hopes for a wedding day and dreams of what it could actually look like. "The beach. Sunset. No fuss, no frills—just you, me, and God. And Jazz and Grams and Dad and Macie—and all of your people too."

"I like the sound of that." Brander hugs me closer and presses his lips to my temple before whispering into my hair. "But when? Tomorrow? Next week?"

"No." My elbow finds his ribs, and I give him a quick jab. "Your mom's right. We have to take some time. But I do *not* want an aquarium dance floor at the reception."

"A what?" Brander pulls away. "Where'd you get an idea like that?"

I jerk my chin toward the Delacroix manor, towering on the hill above Brander's simple studio cottage. "Your mom keeps texting me."

"Maybe we should have another planning meeting, then. You know—get some things straightened out."

"Okay." The thought alone makes my stomach pinch. "When?"

Before Brander can answer, something tap-tap-taps along the pathway leading from Brander's place to the Delacroix house. Something that sounds suspiciously like...

"Now?" Brander whispers under his breath as Midori rounds the corner.

"Olivia? I thought I saw your car in the driveway. Are you joining us for dinner tonight?"

Dread floods through my stomach, making my appetite curdle like I just drank a full gallon jug of vinegar. Not exactly the dinner date I had in mind. I swallow hard and open my mouth, though I haven't quite decided whether it's to accept her invitation or remind her that I only answer to Olive when Brander silences me with a tug on my hand.

"Mom, her name is—"

"Never mind," I cut in, cheeks heating. "Actually, Midori, we were about to head out. We'll catch you later, okay?" I flinch at the sour note in my own voice, but Midori's sudden presence has my brain spinning with half a million unmade decisions—exactly what I *don't* want for this evening.

Midori peers down her nose at me, as if in disapproval, but she flaps a hand like she couldn't care less. "Fine, fine." She turns toward the house, then stops and peers at me. "Olivia, have you been getting my text messages?"

"Yeah." My cheeks grow warm. "Your ideas sound..."

"Mom." Brander tightens his grip on my hand. "I'm glad you're excited, but the logistics of everything can wait. Olive and I need time to celebrate being engaged before we start worrying about details."

"We can't let too much time pass. We need to begin making plans if we want any chance of pulling things together in time."

"Give us a week. Please." I barely stop short of clasping my hands over my chest and begging. "Then we'll talk wedding."

"Fine." Midori must finally realize that she's fighting a losing battle, because she gives a stiff little shrug before retreating up the path. "But in the meantime, I'll start looking into things. You can't expect the wedding of your dreams to plan itself, can you?" Her voice carries on even once she's out of sight, and I lean into Brander's warm, stable embrace, filling my ears with the sound of his heartbeat instead.

This week can't last long enough.

# Chapter Six

"I still don't see why you and Brander need to go house hunting today. The wedding is, like, a million years away." Macie crosses her arms and shoots me an almost-glare from her perch on the counter next to the oven as I get ready to leave.

"Trust me, Mace. I get it." True to her word, Midori stayed quiet and gave me and Brander our week of post-engagement bliss. But she called me—at work, actually—on Monday, bubbling over with plans.

"Then stay here with me." Macie huffs and tugs at a wayward curl.

"I wish I could, but Midori said these condos are priced to sell, and there are only four units left. We need to make a decision before they're all gone."

"But why a condo? Can't you at least stick around long enough to taste-test my chocolate lava cake?"

"Sorry Mace, but Brander's going to be here any minute. Have Jazz come over—you know she'd love a piece." I dip my finger into a bowl full of silky chocolate batter and give it a lick. "But for the record, I think the batter tastes great."

This must be enough to placate her, because she jumps off the counter to give me a hug. "You'll make sure you pick a unit with two bedrooms so I can come over and spend the night, right?"

"Absolutely." I run a hand through Macie's mop of curls but stop when I encounter a tangle.

"Hey! That hurt." Macie pulls away and shoots me the Hawaiian Stink Eye—a look she seems to have perfected as of late. "I knew I should've straightened my hair this morning."

*Why? So it can frizz again in the next five seconds?*

Thankfully Gramma materializes with a question about cocoa powder ratios before that thought can escape via my mouth, and I seize the opportunity to dash out the door before I can further exasperate my little sister.

Outside, I barely have a chance to slip on my shoes before Brander pulls up to the curb, a bouquet of lilies, orchids, and plumeria waiting in the front seat, his parents wedged into the back.

"Good grief." I flop into my seat. "You didn't have to mow down an entire flower field for my sake. But I'm glad you did." I raise the bouquet to my nose and catch a whiff of plumeria, so much like that of Mom's old perfume that it makes my heart swell until it nearly bursts. I lift my eyes to the heavens before saying hello to Brander's parents.

"Ready to go?" Brander's mom taps her sleek smartwatch with one finger and glances at her husband. "Auggie, the Realtor is meeting us in half an hour, correct?"

"That's right, dear." Auggie yanks a handkerchief out of his shirt pocket and wipes his glistening bald head as Brander pulls away from the curb.

"Can you explain this whole thing to me again?" I glance at Midori and Auggie. "You're buying me and Brander a house?" The words taste bitter in my mouth. I have money after all—not a lot, but some. Why aren't Brander and I picking out and buying a house on our own?

"We're not *buying* it for you, dear." Midori folds her hands in her lap and lifts her chin in the air as Auggie clears his throat heartily.

"You and Brander will be doing me a favor. My LLC is looking to expand into vacation rentals and long-term residence options. This complex is our trial run."

*So, in other words, we're your guinea pigs.*

"We're simply acting as a guide." Midori speaks again, as if she has ultrasonic ears that can somehow listen to my deepest thoughts. "To help you make the best choice."

"Isn't that the real estate guy's job?" The tart words slip out before I can stop them. No wonder Macie has picked up an attitude as of late if this is the kind of role model she's living with. "I mean, if Brander and I are doing this on our own..."

"Well, I might pitch in a bit." August shoves the sweat-stained hanky in his pocket. "After all, Brander works for my company. I've always said that the best way to build employee loyalty is to offer them a bonus they can't refuse. Isn't that right, Midori?"

"Absolutely." Something akin to a smile creases her pearly-white cheeks. "Besides, by taking one of the units, Brander will be acting as both a resident and a complex manager—it's a position we wouldn't entrust to just anyone."

"So it's one of his job requirements?"

"If you'd like to think of it that way, then yes." Mrs. Delacroix folds her hands and falls silent. Even still, her usual perfect mask of complacency seems a little skewed today, like there's a different part of her—a secret part—that wants to be let out into the open.

Before I can figure out exactly what that part might be, Brander pulls into the parking garage of a condominium complex a few miles from the resort grounds. It's full of glossy cars with custom plates and fancy-looking hood ornaments. I gulp.

"These units are expensive?" I crack my door and slide out of the car, careful to keep from knocking my hip against a shiny black Lamborghini.

"Only the finest for Delacroix Hospitality. We bought this complex a few years ago. Our design team has been renovating the units to fit our brand. With a lodging option like this, we can offer travelers a more holistically local experience." Auggie points across the parking garage to a massive pool flanked by hibiscus bushes and tiki torches, beyond which lays the glimmering gem of the Pacific. "*And* we're right on the water."

"Right on the water, huh?" I take an extra-long look at the glistening ocean and breathe in a gulp of air that smells a little like saltwater and a lot like chlorine as we head across the parking garage to the elevator.

Maybe this won't be so bad after all.

"I don't think I can do this." I groan and lean against a marble-topped kitchen island. Brander reaches for my hand as we stare across a wide, open-air living space to the ocean, which sparkles like a gem beyond the unit's massive penthouse-level balcony—or *lanai*, as the agent called it.

This is the third unit we've toured, and each one seems better than the rest. It's...perfect. Too perfect, maybe. "I don't see how we'll ever choose."

"You don't?" Mrs. Delacroix makes a tiny sniffing sound—her version of a huff, maybe. "There can't be that much of a question. You should obviously—"

"Midori." August lays a hand on his wife's arm, and she

snaps her mouth shut, looking somewhat like a piranha devouring its prey. "Let the children decide on their own."

I nearly bristle at being called a *child*—I started my own 401k last year, after all—but Brander's hand on my arm keeps me from saying something I'll regret.

Mrs. Delacroix sniff-huffs again and crosses the marble-tiled living space to open the door to the lanai. The sound of crashing waves, accompanied by a gust of hot air, instantly fills the room, and the coil of uncertainty in my chest unravels slightly.

"Remember, no matter which unit we choose, we'll wake up to *that* every morning." Brander's breath tickles my ear as he whispers to me, and a thrill of excitement flies through my chest.

After all, we aren't playing make-believe or looking at these condos for the fun of it. We're actually going to live in one of them—when we're married.

*Married.*

The very thought makes me want to break into song and dance around the room with Brander like I'm the star of an incredibly cheesy Broadway musical. But since I'm currently in the company of my future in-laws—not to mention the real estate agent they brought in—I settle for giving Brander's hand a squeeze instead.

"Well then." Midori's voice knifes through the warm fuzzies that were beginning to form in my chest as she slides the door to the *lanai* shut. It protests with a squeak, and Midori cuts her eyes at August. "Be sure you send someone to get that fixed."

"Yes, dear." Brander's dad pulls out his phone and taps out a note before peering at me and Brander. "You've seen the three suites. Which way are you leaning?"

I shake my head. This is like being stuck in an everlasting episode of *House Hunters*. There's a reason those shows are only a half hour long. "They're all nice, but none of them feel like home." And if none of these posh, perfectly styled masterpieces of modern design feel like home...

Midori opens her mouth, as if to object. But before she can get a word out, the real estate agent raises a hand, as if he's a student waiting to be called on.

"Yes?" Midori peers down her long, flat nose at the man.

"Sorry to interrupt, but there is one more unit. I know it's not quite as impressive as the penthouses, but it's my own personal favorite. If I had the money, I'd snatch it up myself."

"But—"

Midori is silenced with one pointed look from her husband, and Brander shoots the realtor a thumbs-up. "Lead the way."

One long elevator ride later, the five of us huddle in an open-air walkway next to an unassuming paneled door—a far cry from the glass-paned French doors marking the entrance to each of the penthouse suites.

"It's right next to the stairwell." Brander's mother sniffs yet again. "Tourists will be clattering around at all hours of the day and night. You'd never get any sleep."

"Ah, dear, you're forgetting that my construction team specifically took into consideration every aspect of an ideal vacation experience. Each unit has been soundproofed with the best materials on the market." Mr. Delacroix places his hands on Midori's shoulders. "Give it a chance."

Taking that as his cue, the agent unlocks the door and

ushers us inside. We're greeted by a long, dim hallway, and Midori sniffs again.

I step inside first, careful to remove my shoes per the sign hanging from the door, and wander down the hall, slipping into the first room I come to. It's a bedroom—about the size of the one I share with Macie at home—and a window on the far side of the room looks out over a jungle of lush palms and bamboo sticks. Brander appears at my side and nods his approval. So far, so good.

"It's dim in here. And cramped." Midori barely glances at the room before continuing her quest down the hall. The rest of us follow in silence as she delivers a running commentary on the other two rooms—a smaller bedroom and a spacious, well-appointed bathroom—before we reach the living space.

"Lovely, isn't it?" The realtor leans against the wall and motions to the cluster of three palm trees swaying beyond the small *lanai.*

Midori sniffs and folds her arms over her chest. "It's nice enough for a weekend getaway. Any longer in here and you would be a sardine."

I shrug. "I think it's kind of cozy."

Midori shakes her head, and a strand of hair falls across her eyes. It only takes her a second to smooth it back into her perfect coiffure, but for a moment, she almost looks like...Brander. "Who needs cozy in Maui?"

"Me?" It comes out with half the confidence I'd intended, and I bite my lip. Midori is right. The space *is* tiny—only half the size of the penthouse living areas. But, even so, something about it feels safe. Familiar, even.

The kitchen is laid out much the same as Gramma's, and the living space is staged with a brightly patterned couch and two cushy armchairs. It's a far cry from the million-dollar, bohemian-wannabe furnishings in the rooms upstairs, but I like it all the same. Possibly more.

"Well?" The realtor focuses on Brander and me, and that one word is all I need.

"This is it." Brander and I speak at exactly the same time, and even August murmurs his agreement. But Midori's voice is missing from the fray.

"You can't be serious." Her tone is pinched when she finally speaks, and the rest of us sober up quickly. She closes her eyes briefly, and, when she reopens them, her gaze is fixed on me. "You want a corner unit next to the stairwell when you could have a palace fit for a queen?"

"That's exactly it." I smile at Midori so sweetly I'm afraid I'll get cavities, but it will be worth it if I can make her understand. "I'm not a queen, and I'm not sure I'd enjoy living like one either. This place is perfect. It feels like..."

"Home." Brander swoops in, supplying the perfect word for the warm sense of rightness blooming in my chest at the thought of living here. "This one feels like home. To both of us."

"If you're sure..." Midori bites her lip, scraping off a layer of blood-red color, then turns to the realtor. "Let's draw up the papers."

The realtor leaves soon after we've finished filling out a mountain of preliminary paperwork. August and Midori follow him with some lame excuse about checking on the landscaping out front, leaving me and Brander alone in our very own house.

"Our house." I try the words on for size, and they fit

nicely on my tongue. "You're sure you'll be happy here? Your mom was pushing pretty hard for one of those penthouses."

Brander runs a hand through his hair, ruffling his cowlick. "I like this one better than all the others."

"But you grew up living in a—"

Brander brings his finger to my lips, and I fall quiet. "That doesn't mean that's where I want to spend the rest of my life. Wherever your heart is happiest, that's where I'm at home." He takes my hand and leads me out onto the lanai. "I can't think of anywhere else I'd want to start our adventure."

"Me neither." I lean my head against his shoulder and close my eyes. But, before I can get too comfortable, something that's been niggling at the back of my mind jumps to the forefront of my brain. "Uh-oh."

"What?" Brander pulls away to look at me, concern knit into his brow.

"This apartment's awfully small. You're not planning on bringing Rosco with you, are you?"

Brander's eyes grow wide for a moment before they crease around the edges in a smile. "What? No. Rosco's a guard dog, not a house pet. He'd go nuts living in a condo—plus, my mom likes the protection."

*Protection, my foot.* "I figured, but I just wanted to...never mind." I'm laughing now, and Brander's throaty chuckle joins my giggles to create a concert of laughter that mingles with the sound of ocean waves crashing against the rocky seawall.

But all too soon, something else fills my ears—the memory of Midori's voice earlier, rising in objection to my choice of a condo. Will she act the same way when Brander and I tell her about our dream of a sunset wedding ceremony on the beach—*not* an elaborate affair at the resort?

The knots in my chest that had begun to loosen earlier clench into an even bigger tangle of nerves. "Um, so..." The rest of the words—and there are a lot of them—catch in my throat. Though maybe that's for the best.

After all, Midori is Brander's mother—and my future mother-in-law. I guess, according to the Bible, that means I'm supposed to honor her.

But how can I honor Midori's dreams when they're shaping up to be my definition of a nightmare?

# Chapter Seven

NEXT WEDNESDAY AT WORK, MY PHONE buzzes with a text right as I submit my final article of the day—a snoozer about how tourists can find the elusive Hawaiian monk seal. Spoiler alert—you probably can't.

I texted Brander this morning about biting the bullet and scheduling another meeting of the infamous wedding-planning committee, and I've been waiting to hear back before I decide whether or not it's is a good time to go into all-out bridezilla mode.

I pull out my phone and take a peek—not Brander.

Jazz.

**Can you give me a ride tonight?**

I bite my lip. Work might be over for the day, but I have a miniature Mount Haleakala of laundry teetering in my hamper back home. Still, given a choice between Jazz and the washing machine... **What's up?**

**It's Wednesday.**

I text back with a string of question marks before it clicks—youth group. **Sure I can!**

Jazz responds with a smiley face with stars in its eyes. **Hunter and Brander are doing worship—don't want to miss that.**

*Huh.*

Hunter again.

The corners of my mouth twitch. Whether Jazz realizes it or not, Hunter is totally smitten—and maybe Jazz is too.

There's no chance on earth I'm going to miss out on a chance to see those two together. Besides, with the combination of work boredom and wedding-planning stress that's hanging over my head, a dose of Jesus—and a plate full of Pirate Pete's Pizza—is exactly what I need.

That laundry will have to wait.

By the time I show up at Jazz's place, I've changed out of my work clothes and into my favorite jean shorts and a rainbow-colored t-shirt reminding people—myself included—to "live aloha". This might be because it's one of my favorite outfits, or it might be because it's one of the few things *not* spilling out of my dirty clothes hamper. Possibly both.

"Thanks for picking me up." Jazz cracks open the passenger door and lowers herself inside. The hem of her filmy white maxi dress lifts to reveal her metal prosthesis, glinting in the late-afternoon sunlight. A strange look flicks over her face, and she tugs at her skirt to cover her leg. "I love having friends with wheels."

Technically Jazz, Brander, and I should have aged out of youth group when we started college, but somehow we became the group's honorary older siblings. It makes sense for Brander and Jazz—they have enough Gramma-instilled wisdom to help solve any teenage dilemma. I, on the other hand...

Well, I'm learning. Until then, I'm a great example of what *not* to do. And I make for great comic relief.

*Ha.*

"So...it sounds like you and Hunter were talking again." I keep one eye fixed on Jazz as I pull onto Front Street, but she turns her head and stares out the window like she's never seen the cobblestone-fronted seaman's hospital before in her life.

"We weren't *talking*. We were texting." Jazz's voice straddles a narrow line between playful and petulant.

"Well, excuse me. What were you texting about?"

"He had a question about the paperwork."

"Paperwork?" I tear my gaze from Jazz to keep an eye on the crosswalk. A tourist family made up of what appear to be multiple pairs of twins tootles across the street. "You gave it to him forever ago. Isn't he done with it yet?"

"No." Even without looking directly at Jazz, I tell the exact moment when her spine stiffens. "Olive, it's a *lot* of paperwork."

"Okay, okay." It's all I can do to keep from laughing, and I choose my next words with care. "I still don't get what that paperwork has to do with you asking if he'd be at youth group."

"It wasn't like that!" I look over at Jazz in time to catch her cheeks turning a shade darker than the red hibiscus bush in Gramma's yard. "I mean..."

"It's okay to like him, you know." My voice goes dead serious as the family finally finishes crossing the road and we continue on our way down Front Street, but I lighten it for my next attempt. "There's still time to plan a double wedding."

"What? No!" Jazz's words are so forceful that they're anything but convincing. "Hunter's nice and all, but he's a big goober with an overgrown manbun. Besides, he isn't ready to think about settling down right now. He doesn't even have a real job."

"Wait, what? Wasn't he..."

"He quit working the Shave Ice Shack to spend more

time helping with the youth ministry and booking gigs for the band. Besides..." She ducks her head and readjusts her skirt.

"What?"

"Nothing." But her suddenly soft tone and the downward slant to her lips assure me that it is *something*. "Hey, what ever happened to the aquarium dance floor?"

"Changing the subject much?"

Jazz lifts a shoulder, and I sigh in defeat. "I haven't heard anything about the aquarium floor in a while, but Midori and I are going to get together again soon to talk about her precious details. It'll probably come up then. I wish I had some backup."

"What's Brander? Overripe breadfruit? He should be able to handle his own mom." Jazz lays a finger alongside her chin as I pull into the church parking lot. "But if you're *that* concerned about it, you could always have your lovely maid of honor tag along for moral support."

"You'd do that?" I maneuver my way into a parking space, then turn to Jazz and clasp my hands over my chest. "You're a lifesaver!"

"Whoa now, are you asking me to be your maid of honor?" Jazz fans her face like she's flattered, but there's a playful twinkle in her eyes as we climb out of the car. "What makes you think I'll say yes?"

"Because you wouldn't miss an opportunity to wear a fancy dress—or help plan a party—for anything." I start toward the church pavilion, but Jazz stops me with a tug on my hand. "What?"

Before I know what's happening, Jazz is wrapping her arms around me and hugging so tight it's all I can do to disentangle my arms and hug her back.

"You're the best friend in the world, Olive." Jazz finally releases her grip and looks at me, silvery eyes sparkling a little more than usual in the afternoon sunlight. Something about the way she's staring at me makes my own eyes water a little. I blink at the fraying hem of my shorts, my throat suddenly thick. A bird trills somewhere in the distance as I look back at Jazz. I see her face now, then I see it a thousand times over.

Smiling like a crazed Cheshire Cat the day she stood on Gramma's front porch—ambushing me when we were total strangers.

Grinning triumphantly the day she stood for the first time on her prosthesis.

Beaming at me with tears in her eyes as Brander and I exchange our rings some day in the not-too-distant future...

"Hey, dudes!" A voice splits through the tropical concerto of bird chirps—*and* my daydream.

I glance up in time to watch Hunter throw his battered drumsticks up in the air and catch them neatly behind his back. He flashes one fist in a shaka, then uses his sticks to salute us as he jogs closer, a goofy grin on his face.

"Aloha!" Jazz waves back, her tone even perkier than normal. "Nice moves."

Before Hunter can attempt to impress us with any more drumstick acrobatics, his phone cuts him off with a slightly urgent-sounding chirp. He digs in the pocket of his oversized board shorts, pulls out his phone, and glares at the screen. "Olive, your fiancé is turning into a major flake."

"Huh?" I stand at attention—though whether it's from hearing Hunter refer to Brander as my fiancé or a major flake, I'm not exactly sure. "What are you talking about?"

"He bailed on me."

"No way." Jazz shakes her head, sending her braid whipping out until it almost swats Hunter in the arm. "You must've read it wrong."

"Nope." Hunter shakes his head, and half of his hair slides loose from its elastic. He holds up the phone so both Jazz and I can read: **Can't make it tonight. Cover for me?**

"Not much room for error." Hunter peers at us over his phone screen as he taps out a response, then slides the phone into his pocket.

Something akin to heartburn—except a lot more fiery and definitely self-inflicted—stirs in my chest. "That doesn't mean he's a flake. Something could be wrong."

"Yeah, like the fact that I have to make it through the set on my own. I haven't picked up a guitar in months." He shakes his head and starts toward the pavilion. Jazz follows, offering a stream of encouragement, her shoulder close to Hunter's own. There's definitely a spark between them. But what does that matter now?

I take a few steps forward, my halfhearted pace no match for Jazz and Hunter's power stride. I only make it as far as the pavilion steps before I stop and dig out my phone to text Brander myself:

**What's wrong? Where are you?**

The text delivers instantly, so I sit on the pavilion steps while I wait for him to respond. But minutes pass with no answer—not even a little "seen" icon to assure me that Brander hasn't completely fallen off the face of the earth. Because that's the only reason I can think of that he would decide to bail on Hunter at the last minute. Especially since Hunter can't sing.

Like, at all.

"That was rough." Hunter runs a hand over what must be at least a week's worth of growth on his chin as we get in line to load our plates with Pirate Pete's pizza—the best on the island—after worship. "Olive, you might want to talk to Brander and let him know that bailing on your bandmates is *not* cool."

*Especially when said bandmate sounds like a cat that's been stuck in the gutter for a month.* No one says that part aloud, but it's obvious that's what he means.

It's all I can do to sit through dinner and the sermon, plus hang around afterwards to talk with the others before heading out. As soon as I've dropped Jazz off at the rescue—probably earlier than she'd like—I put my phone on speaker and dial Brander's number.

"Hey." Brander's voice comes on, smooth and easy. I open my mouth to ask what on earth happened to him, but— "You've reached Brander Delacroix, the lead singer of Anchor. If you'd like to speak with me about business matters regarding Delacroix Hospitality, please hang up and dial..."

The recording keeps blaring in my ear, but it's drowned out by the sudden swarm of thoughts buzzing in my head. I can count on a closed fist the number of times Brander has willingly let my call go to voicemail.

Something must be *really* wrong.

Even though I'm already halfway home, I whip out a U-turn and head straight for Brander's place. Fifteen minutes and several broken traffic laws later, I screech to a halt in front of the Delacroix mansion, hop out of the car, and half-jog down the path to Brander's studio.

All of the lights are off, but that doesn't stop me from dashing up the front steps and banging on the door.

Nothing.

I try the doorbell once. Then again.

Still nothing.

Fear grows, icy and cold, in the pit of my stomach as I pull out my phone to see if he's read my message.

Nada.

I sink onto the steps and rest my chin in my hands. *God, I don't know where Brander is or what's wrong, but please let him be okay.*

And that's when I hear them. Footsteps.

"Olivia?" I cringe at the sound of the name that only one person in the world could get away with calling me, but I clamber to my feet as Midori Delacroix rounds the corner, a lime green mud mask smeared across her normally ivory-colored face. I must have interrupted her nightly beautification routine. "I almost thought you were a burglar. What are you doing out here?"

*I only answer to Olive, thank you very much.* I open my mouth to tell Midori as much, then stop. Why bother correcting her when there are greater things at stake? Besides, a tiny part of my heart can't help but admit that hearing that name agin is strangely...never mind. "Where's Brander? Is he okay?"

Midori narrows her eyes, almost in slow motion, and the hardening gook smeared on her face crackles around the edges. "Of course he's okay. Why wouldn't he be?"

"If he's okay, then where *is* he?"

"At work. With August." Midori stares at me like I've grown a coconut where my brain should be. "The resort has been asked to host a highly exclusive orthopedic convention this January. Normally August would take care of the arrangements on his own, but he wanted Brander to stay and see how it's done. Get some experience."

"You mean he's...*working*? This late? He was supposed to lead worship for youth group tonight."

Midori flaps a hand in the air, waving away my protest as if it's nothing more than a pesky mosquito. "This is a major client. If Brander and Auggie book this convention, it'll bring in enough revenue to pay their salary for half a year." Midori's face softens as much as it can, considering the constraints of the green clay mask. "You do realize, dear—the hotel business waits for no one."

*Not even God?* I bite my lip. Something about this whole situation seems kind of fishy—and I'm not talking about the seaweed smell emanating from Midori's spa mask. "Do you have any idea when he'll be home?"

Midori shrugs in a movement so fluid she looks more like a famous ballerina than a middle-aged mom. "Hasn't Brander told you the stories? There were days when Auggie used to spend the night at the office. I wouldn't see him for days when he was in the middle of a project like this."

I swallow hard, but something in my throat keeps anything from going down. "You mean August slept at the office?"

"Not slept, dear. Worked." Mrs. Delacroix raises a hand to scratch her nose and comes away with a finger full of greenish goop. She stares at her hand for a moment, then lowers it gingerly, keeping it far away from her silky white lounge pants. "If you'd like to wait for him, I'm sure he'd appreciate it. But I'll warn you—it might be a while."

# Chapter Eight

I manage to make it—sitting on the cold, hard steps in front of Brander's place after Midori goes inside to wash off her mask—until midnight. By then, my yawns have become so frequent I feel like I'm doing jaw calisthenics and Brander *still* hasn't seen my texts, so I throw in the towel and head home.

By the time I manage a quick shower and creep into bed, it's close to one o'clock. My eyelids can barely stay open, but I can't help but wonder—if I'm this tired, how must Brander be feeling right now?

"Olive. Olive!" The next thing I know, I'm hit with the bright blaze of early-morning sun and Macie is shaking me awake. Her flat ironed hair is neatly collected into two ponytails, and an overstuffed backpack hangs from her shoulders. "Wake up! I missed the bus and Grams is already at the gallery. You have to take me to school."

I prop myself up on one elbow and stare at her. "School? I never take you to school. I'm usually..." What am I usually doing? I scrub my eyes and yawn. I'm usually...

*Oh no.*

I never take Macie to school, because I'm usually on my way to work. "What time is it?" I don't wait for an answer before throwing myself out of bed and stumbling to the closet to throw on a dress.

"It's *time* to *go!*" Macie wails behind me as I take off for the bathroom at a dead sprint.

After the quickest face-washing, tooth-brushing routine in history, I meet Macie in the kitchen and drag her out to my car like we're practicing for a tsunami-evacuation drill.

"Careful! You'll mess up my hair." Macie wrenches away and smooths a hand over both of her ponytails as she flops into the front passenger seat. "I already had to straighten it twice this morning. *That's* why I missed the bus."

"Figures." I pull out of the driveway, trying my hardest to keep from looking at the clock on my dashboard. I don't even *want* to know how late I'm going to be. "Why do you even try? You have the same hair as I do, except darker."

"So?" Macie crosses her arms and sinks into her seat.

"*So* it'll never stay straight. Not in this humidity." I flick on the air conditioner and get hit in the face with a blast of disappointingly *not*-cold air.

"Olive!" Macie wails and hurries to close both of the vents on her side. "What is *wrong* with you this morning? I know you're a spaz, but this is a whole new level."

*Gee, thanks a lot, Mace.* Everything in me is itching to say exactly that. But like the mature, rational older sister that I am—yeah, right—I take a deep breath and tell her about my night.

"He bailed on youth group? Well, I never thought I'd see the day." The words—far more likely to come from Gramma's mouth yet delivered in Macie's sassy tone—bring a smile to my face as I turn down the road to her school.

"What do you think I should do about it?"

"You're asking *me* for relationship advice? All I know

about boys is that all the ones at school still think I have cooties. You should ask Dad. He's a guy, after all."

"True." I murmur the word under my breath as I pull in to the drop-off zone, but my stomach lets out a ferocious growl, effectively drowning out my response. Leave it to me to forget to grab food for the road. Or my lunch from the fridge.

Macie must take pity on me, because she reaches into her backpack and pulls out two jumbo, white chocolate macadamia nut cookies and hands them to me. "Here. So your coworkers don't think you're hiding a pit bull under your shirt."

The thought of a growling pit bull—or any growling dog, for that matter—still makes me a little nauseous, but I'm so hungry I don't care. I take the cookies and shove half of one into my mouth. "Thanks, Mace—you're the best," I mumble around the mouthful.

"You can give me the money later." She opens her door and hops out of the front seat, pigtails bouncing.

"Wait...money?"

"Yeah. Those are for the bake sale today. Five bucks each." She offers a shiny smile before disappearing into the crowd of kids.

I shake my head but can't help smiling as I pull onto the street and head for work—over an hour late. I'll be typing through my lunch break, but at least that's not as bad as staying at the office until after midnight. Or missing youth group.

Did Brander *ever* make it home?

I punch the button on my steering wheel to activate my phone's Bluetooth connection and give him a call, but it doesn't work. I do a quick dig through my purse during a red light but come up empty-handed.

My phone must still be at home...along with my lunch. Oh, yeah. This day can't get much better.

Three traffic jams, two road work sites, and one chicken who makes it halfway across the road only to discover he didn't want to get to the other side after all have made me almost *two* hours late by the time I finally walk through the door to the office. Mark, my boss, shoots me a look, but the phone pressed to his ear is enough to keep him from saying anything as I walk by.

The workday goes by in a whirlwind. By the time I've put in an extra hour on my column to make up for my tardiness, my head aches like someone tried to zap my eyes with a laser. I haven't gotten up from my desk all day—a fact I'm sorely reminded of when I finally stand to leave.

I hobble out to the parking lot, feeling more like someone Gramma's age than a normal twenty-one-year-old, and the late-afternoon sunlight filtering through the overhead palm trees makes my head hurt even worse.

I'm halfway across the parking lot when a horn beeps— practically in my ear, sending another lightning bolt of pain through my head. I massage my temples before turning to find a familiar cherry-red Porsche idling behind me.

"Brander!" Last night's frustration with him *almost* forgotten, I fling myself into the passenger's seat and give his shoulder a playful punch. "Did you finally get out of prison?" I'm a little louder than I intend to be, especially considering that Brander chooses that exact moment to cut the motor. A group of tourists walking by turns to stare, and my cheeks grow painfully hot.

Brander simply laughs and leans over to give me a kiss. "You didn't answer your phone all day. What's wrong?"

"I could ask you the same thing, you know." I give his arm another shove, then let my hand travel down to squeeze his own. "What'd your dad do? Lock you in the office? I was waiting for you at your place until midnight."

"Oh, man." Brander drops his head, but not before I can get a good look at the deep, dark bags beneath his eyes. "I'm sorry. I started to text you, but then I got another call and..."

"What was so important that you had to miss youth group? You totally bailed on everyone, and Hunter...I mean, he's a great guy and all that, but—"

"He can't sing." Brander shakes his head. "I know. He called me this morning on his way to work. Singing."

"Ouch."

"He got the point across. I shouldn't have canceled like that, but Dad...it's no excuse." The regret on Brander's face is almost palpable, and a sliver of guilt wedges itself into my chest. After all, it's not like Auggie asked Brander to renounce his faith or anything.

I give his hand a squeeze. "Don't get upset. There's no harm done." *Unless you count a few busted eardrums.* "What do you say we go grab some sushi?"

"Actually, we're supposed to meet Jonah at Kimo's, remember?" Brander motions for me to buckle up and puts the car in drive. "I texted you this morning..."

"No phone, remember?" My excitement at seeing Brander fizzles a bit at the thought of another session with Jonah.

"Right." Brander shakes his head and drums his fingers against the steering wheel. "Does that work for you? If not, we can reschedule."

"Yeah. It works." The words taste like cardboard on my tongue, though. So much for a relaxing evening.

I give myself a shake as Brander pulls out of the parking lot. After all, there's nothing *wrong* with premarital counseling. Especially now that this relationship is starting to feel a bit like a love triangle. One with Brander's parents—and that job of his—right in the middle.

Unfortunately, the counseling session ends up taking a completely different turn. By the time our waiter brings out two monster slices of Kimo's famous "hula pie"—one for Jonah, one for me and Brander to split—Brander and I are now fully prepared with an arsenal of everything we ever need to know about each other's love languages—and everything we don't. *Go figure.*

"Anything else you'd like to talk about tonight?" Jonah dips his jumbo spork, imprinted with the Kimos's hula pie logo, into his slice.

I open my mouth to say...what, exactly? How can I explain what's going on without making Mrs. Delacroix sound like a mini Napoleon and me like a major control freak? I sit there, mouth hanging open like I'm a hungry sea turtle, for so long that Brander ends up popping a forkful of chocolate-cloaked ice cream pie into my mouth—a welcome substitute for my half-formed question.

I'm still reveling in that bite of chocolate heaven when a forceful buzz rattles Brander's leg—the one pressed against my own in the restaurant booth. I nearly jump out of my seat. "Good grief, what was that?"

Brander pulls out his phone and stares at the screen. Not a local number. "My dad said the coordinator for that orthopedic convention might call this evening. Can I take this real quick?"

Barely waiting for an answer, Brander slips out of his seat and ducks over to an empty place at the restaurant's balcony railing. He presses the phone close to his face but turns his head so I can't make out his expression.

"This could take a while." I motion to Jonah's rapidly-melting slice of pie. "Better not let all this ice cream get away from us."

Jonah and I share a conspiratorial grin as we dig into our slices. We're silent for a few moments, lost somewhere in the land of chocolate-macadamia-nut goodness, before Jonah clears his throat. "You seemed pretty quiet at youth group yesterday. Is something wrong?"

"Kind of."

"Hmm." Jonah shovels another spoonful of pie into his mouth. "What's up?"

Before I can tell Jonah about Brander's job *or* Mrs. Delacroix's dream-wedding-turned-nightmare, Brander reappears at the table, an inscrutable look transforming his face. Reminding me of...something. "You'll never guess who that was."

"We won't?" Jonah and I share a glance.

"Never."

"I guess you should tell us then, huh?" I scan Brander's face for a clue. He's smiling, so it can't be bad news, but there's something in his eyes that spells *t-r-o-u-b-l-e*. I tense as Brander reclaims his spoon and retrieves a mega-sized bite of pie.

"Guys, Mike Parker's record label wants to sign Anchor."

"What?" The word comes out in a near-shriek, and half the people in the restaurant turn to stare. Leave it to me to make a scene just by being human.

"Anchor! The band. He wants to sign us." Brander looks like he's about to either break into song or pass out. I can't quite tell which, even though I know exactly what *I* feel like doing—and it definitely doesn't involve singing. He eventually flops into his seat before continuing. "Mike said he's been keeping tabs on us for a while now, and the label's looking to sign a duo. This is our big break—Hunter's gonna flip."

"Hunter?" I can practically feel my eyeballs popping out of their sockets. "What about your fiancée? She's flipping out. Right now."

"Me too!" Brander jumps up, pulling me right alongside him, and wraps me in a hug before lifting me and spinning me around. The rest of the people in the restaurant cheer and clap like they're at a theater or something. My cheeks grow hot as Brander releases me and we both drop into our chairs. But while Brander is beaming, something is stirring beneath the surface of my own strained smile.

The last time Brander got mixed up with Mike Parker, I thought for sure I'd lose my best friend to the lure of shining lights, screaming crowds, and everything else on the mainland. Now, when I didn't think things could get any crazier...

"This is *crazy*." Brander plants his hands on the table, his face brimming with such excitement like he's ready to burst into laughter or tears of joy. Or both. "Crazy!"

"And I think you'd be *crazy* to accept." The words pop out of my mouth without any warning, but I hardly regret them. Not when they ring so true.

"What?" It takes a moment for Brander to respond and, when he does, the excitement drains from his countenance. His whole face falls. His eyes dim. His cheeks grow pale. "Why?"

"Aren't you and Hunter doing fine on your own? Do you seriously want to be flying to the mainland all the time for tours and stuff? And we can't pick up and move to *Nashville*. We have jobs here. A house. *Ohana*."

"Who said anything about moving?" Brander's forehead crinkles. "I thought you'd be excited about this."

"Sorry. I—you're right. I should be excited." *But I'm not.* I don't say it out loud, but it still must show on my face if Brander's falling expression is anything to go by. A flicker of guilt joins the hula pie in my stomach, but I can't force a smile. After all, how can I embrace the very thing that's threatening to tear me and Brander apart?

# Chapter Nine

"I STILL CAN'T BELIEVE BRANDER AND Hunter got a record deal. Just like that!" Jazz snaps her fingers as Gramma maneuvers her station wagon into a parking spot in front of a small, white-painted building with black-and-white striped awnings—the Ma'ema'e Bridal Boutique.

"Tell me about it." I smother what is definitely a groan—yet shouldn't be—and lean against the seat. Isn't wedding dress shopping supposed to be fun? We haven't even started and I'm already exhausted. Possibly because Mrs. Delacroix planned the whole trip after her housekeeper's sister Eve, who works at Ma'ema'e, caught wind of the big wedding to-do. Supposedly Eve and Abigail ganged up to convince Midori that this is the *only* boutique on the island with dresses good enough for the likes of a Delacroix wedding. At least, that's Midori's take on it. "Haven't we been through this all once before?"

When a video clip of Brander's singing went viral a few years back, Brander moved to Nashville for several months, working with Mike to record a single and traveling across the country as part of a national tour. That time, he ended up choosing island life over the Nashville rat race, but now he'll have to decide again. And now the choice isn't on Brander alone—Hunter has an equal say in it.

My stomach clenches. If Brander accepts the deal, where will that leave me—*us?*

"Need an oxygen tank?" Jazz reaches out to take my

hand. "You're two breaths away from totally hyperventilat-ing."

I breathe in deep and turn to look at Jazz, doing my best to ignore Macie's prying gaze from where she's riding shot-gun with Grams. "I know. I'm probably overreacting. But when I said I wanted to marry Brander, I wanted to marry *him*, you know? Not his band." Or his job. Or his helicopter mother, for that matter.

"But...Brander isn't Brander without his music." Macie—the little eavesdropper—peeks at me from her van-tage point in the front passenger's seat.

My stomach folds in on itself as Grams twists the keys in the ignition. The car motor goes silent, and suddenly all I can hear is a continuous-loop playlist of all the crabby, whiny, stupid things I've said and thought over the last few weeks. For a girl whose dreams are all coming true, I sure haven't been acting like it.

"If I may..." Grams turns from her seat in the front and lays a hand on my knee. *Two eavesdroppers?* "I have some-thing for you that might help. I'd planned on saving it until you found 'the dress'..." her arthritic fingers bend in a clumsy attempt at air quotes. "But maybe this would be bet-ter for you to read right now." She digs into her overflowing tote bag of endless wonders and hands me an envelope, yel-lowed with age and creased in several places.

"Thanks." I take it and turn it over. Blank—both sides, except for my name on the front in loopy, lopsided calligra-phy. "What is it?"

"A little note from someone who loves you very much. Macie? Jazz?" Gramma motions to them. "Let's give Olive some space. I hear this boutique has complimentary cup-cakes for all of their customers."

"I bet you they aren't half as good as mine." Macie turns up her nose, but the promise of free sugar draws both her and Jazz out of the car.

"Come in when you're ready, Olive." Gramma reaches back to pat my knee before stepping out and closing the car door.

For a moment, I stay there, frozen despite the sun beating through the car window, staring at the envelope like I should know what's inside—should feel *something*.

When no burst of recognition alights within me, I take a breath and slide my finger under the envelope flap, tearing it just enough to pull out what's inside. The paper is yellow too, and there's something else—a photo.

*Mom.*

My eyes well up at the sight of her, dressed in her own wedding gown. I trace her brilliant white smile with one shaky finger before unfolding the paper.

*Dear Olive,*

My breath catches in my throat, and I swallow hard against a sob.

*If you're reading this, then congratulations!! You've found the dress—and, more importantly, the man—of your dreams. I'm so happy for you, sweet girl, and I wish with all my heart that I could be there with you.*

I blink hard and fast to keep Mom's slanted scrawl from blurring as tears pool in my eyes, then read on. At first, it's all about Mom's own dress and where she found it and how she felt when she first tried it on—she always was a bit long-winded—but then...

*You've probably figured out by now that, though there is most definitely a perfect dress, there's no such thing as a perfect man. When I married your dad, I knew he wasn't perfect.*

*He knew the same about me. We made the choice to love each other because we knew that real, true love is far greater than perfection. When we say we love someone, we're committing ourselves and our hearts not only to them but also to their entire world.*

*I chose to love your dad and his father, mother, and sister. I chose to love his job, even though he was barely making ends meet as an adjunct professor. I chose to love every part of him. And he loved every part of me in return.*

I finish the letter, then close my eyes and let it slip from my hand. Mom's words replay in my head as the haunted look on Brander's face from when I saw him last taunts me. I made it pretty clear what I thought of that record…without even giving him a chance to celebrate his excitement.

I have to call him. Have to apologize. To let him know that, not for the first time, I was wrong.

"Hey." He picks up on the first ring, and the simple sound of his voice is enough to bring more tears to my eyes. "Aren't you supposed to be trying on wedding dresses?"

"Congratulations. On the record deal. I never said that, but I mean it. I'm sorry I freaked out the way I did." I clear my throat and swallow. These next words will be the hardest. "I want you to know that, no matter what you decide, I'm with you a hundred percent. Even if that means moving to Nashville."

"You…are?"

"Yeah. I've been pretty awful lately, and I—well, I'm working on it. I love you and I want to be the girl you deserve, not…you know. A brat."

"You're not a brat."

"Oh, come on. We both know I am."

Brander's laughter bubbles in my ear. "I love you too,

Olive. A lot."

For a moment I can't do anything but sit there, letting Brander's words wrap around me. Feeling their warm embrace. Knowing that I'm loved.

And then someone raps on the car window. I turn my head and find a pair of hawk-like eyes fixed on me. *Midori.*

"What are you doing sitting in that car on a hot afternoon like today—and where are the others?" Her voice is muffled by the car door, and for a moment I feel like a fish stuck in an aquarium. "You'd better not be sweating, or they might not let you try on any of their clothes." Midori shakes her head as I climb out of the car and say a hasty goodbye to Brander.

I open my mouth, ready to assure Midori that my antiperspirant works like a charm, not that it's any of her business, then stop. I love Brander—that much I know. And if loving him means loving his family, then that's what I'm going to do.

Starting now.

I should've started tomorrow.

It's been hours since Eve welcomed us into the private bridal suite. Or at least it feels that way. Midori seems convinced that it's *her* job to singlehandedly select the perfect dress. Which it was—when *she* got married.

So far, we've kept Eve running back and forth between the hangers like a hamster stuck in a ball. Midori turns up her nose at every dress I suggest, vetoing most of them before the poor saleslady can even get them off the hanger. Then, before I can speak up, Midori sends Eve running in the opposite direction—toward a dress that *I* veto just as quickly. Not even the free cupcakes can sweeten Midori up. Especially since they really *aren't* as good as Macie's.

"I don't see what the problem is." Midori crosses the room to feel the fabric on a huge, satiny ball gown. The skirt is so wide I don't see how whoever's wearing it could even fit through a door. "These gowns are all so gorgeous. Why can't you decide?"

"Because she doesn't *like* any of them. And she also has this thing called a budget." Jazz walks over to where Midori is stroking the dress like it's a sleeping kitten. Without another word, Jazz grabs Midori's arm and practically drags her over to a rack of bohemian-style, more realistically priced dresses. The ones I keep going back to—the ones that Eve told us were designed specifically for beach weddings.

"But I—"

"Jazz is right." Macie jumps to her feet and pitches her cupcake wrapper in a white marble wastepaper bin before joining Jazz and Midori at the rack. "You already had your dream wedding. Give Olive her turn. If you don't like how it turns out, then go renew your vows or something."

Midori's eyes grow wide. Very, very wide. She stares at Macie for a second before letting out the faintest of huffs and turning to me, her eyes carrying a hint of apology. "Do what you feel is best, dear." She shakes her head, then crosses back over to her bloated Cinderella costume. "But at least promise me you'll try this one. Before making the final decision."

"Promise." Macie, Jazz, and I say it in unison and even Gramma nods along. Midori groans, as if in defeat, and sinks into a plush white-velvet settee.

"Let the games begin." Jazz flashes me a wicked smile, and that's when the melee ensues. She runs to grab a satiny sort of slip dress that looks more like a straitjacket than something I'd want to say my I do's in. "What about this?"

"No." Macie and I say it together, then crack up laughing.

Even Eve, who has the same wide-mouthed, joyful smile as her sister, joins in. Her silky brown ponytail bounces as she combs through the rack of beach wedding dresses. "You said the ceremony is on the beach, right?"

Midori speaks up before I can. "We haven't actually—"

"Yes. We have." A sudden burst of boldness—minus those warm fuzzy feelings from earlier—takes over. I stand a little taller.

"When did this come about?" Midori's face is pinched.

"Brander and I talked it over. We want to get married on the beach. At sunset. And then..." Inspiration—plus a few returning warm fuzzies—strikes. "Then you can throw us a big, fancy, blowout reception at your resort. We can even do the aquarium dance floor if you want."

Midori's eyes grow as wide as coconuts, cracking the hardened veneer of perfection that usually covers her face. "You're sure?" Her voice is light and breathy. Almost...happy. She smiles. "You want me to plan it?"

"Why not? If you want to give us a party, you can give us a party." A bit of confidence lands in my chest. "But Brander and I have executive veto power, okay?"

Midori nods, slowly at first, then faster. "Yes, of course."

"Great."

We all stand there after that, staring at one another in the happy, semi-awkward silence until Eve claps her hands together and says brightly, "So? A beach wedding?"

This time, we're all in agreement.

Finally, there are only two options left in the running, neither of which look anything like Midori's chosen flounces-and-fluff monstrosity.

The six of us stand in a row, silently surveying the final two contenders. Even though Midori's nose is crinkled slightly—I doubt she's much a fan of either dress—I have to give it to her for trying. She hasn't so much as flinched at any of the dresses I've tried on. Not even Macie's tradition-snubbing pick, a blue ombre dress with layers of chiffon that looked sort of like ocean waves.

"I still think mine should be in the running." Macie huffs and shoves a frizzy chunk of hair behind her ear. "I mean, these two dresses are so *basic*. When I get married, I'm showing up in a hot pink flapper dress."

Midori visibly shudders at that, and I reach over to give Macie's hand a squeeze. "I have no doubt that you'll pull it off Mace, but there's no way I could."

"Fine." Macie pulls away and flops onto the settee. "Then pick one of these so we can get out of here. I'm *starving*."

I fix my eyes on the dresses again. "Jazz? You're the fashion queen here."

Jazz stays silent as she surveys the two choices—a tiered white eyelet gown with three-quarter-length sleeves and a square neckline that makes me feel like a character from *Pride and Prejudice,* and a strappy ivory A-line with a low back and long, lacy train. "Try this one on again." She points to the one on the left, the one with the thin straps and flowing train.

I do as I'm told, closing my eyes for a moment as I approach the mirror. When I open them, I almost gasp. Even though I tried the dress on earlier, seeing it again, nearly glowing in the liquid-gold Hawaiian sunlight, is...different. "This is the one." I strike a pose in the mirror before turning to smile at Gramma and Jazz.

But instead of returning my smile, they both turn to each other with wide, weepy eyes.

"Oh, *no*. Come on, guys, don't look like that." A lump rises in my throat, and a snippet of Mom's letter weaves its way through my mind: *Sweet girl, you'll be the most beautiful bride there ever was.* "Seriously, you guys are gonna make me cry."

"But it's so *perfect*." Jazz practically wails the words as she throws herself into my arms as she does. "You look amazing, Olive." Her whispered words are soft in my ear.

"Brander won't be able to believe his eyes." Gramma's voice is warm and fuzzy, like a flannel blanket on a chilly night. Her arms wrap around me from behind, crushing me into a sandwich-style hug that I wish could last forever.

But eventually enough is enough, and I'm afraid I really *will* start to cry right there in front of Midori and Eve and the rest of the boutique staff. "Come on, guys. You'll ruin the dress." I brush them both off, then turn to take one final glance at myself in the mirror.

The big day can't come soon enough.

*Except...*

A cocky little voice that sounds a bit like Midori tickles my ear as I pull my normal clothes on, reminding me of everything else there is left to plan—food, decor, color scheme.

*...maybe it can.*

# Chapter Ten

"SO, MACE." I KNOCK MY KNEE against Macie's under the dinner table later that night. She's been strangely quiet ever since I vetoed her waterfall-train dress idea, and I've known my sister long enough to know that silence from her usually spells *trouble*. "Do you think Brander'll like the dress?"

"I guess." She drags her fork through her fried rice, pushing out the peas as she goes along. "He probably likes you better in your shorts, though."

"My shorts? Ouch." *Thanks, Mace.*

"I didn't mean it like that." She shakes her head of freshly straightened hair, which is already starting to frizz a bit, and stabs at a piece of General Tso's chicken. "But usually you wouldn't wear a dress like that for a million bucks. It's weird that you're all excited about it."

"Why wouldn't I be excited? It's my wedding dress." I snag a piece of sushi with my chopsticks and pop the whole thing in my mouth. "Kind of a once-in-a-lifetime deal, you know?"

"Trust me, I know." Macie plops her chin on her hand and scoots lower in her chair. "It's all you talk about anymore—getting married. That and your boring, stupid job."

I duck my head and poke at my last piece of sushi with my chopsticks. "I didn't realize—"

"Realize it." Macie drops her fork to her plate with a clatter and scoots away from the table. "Grams, can I be excused?"

"Seeing as how you've already excused yourself, I think that can be arranged." Grams flashes my sister a look tinged with stink eye, and Macie practically runs out of the room and up the stairs. A second later, a door slams and water starts running overhead.

"Do I talk about the wedding that much?" I push away the rest of my sushi.

"You've been talking about it a goodly amount." Gramma slides her chair closer and puts her hand over mine. "As does every bride-to-be. Give Macie time. This is a big adjustment for her."

I stare at Gramma like she's nuts. "For her? She's not the one who has to plan an entire wedding and learn to get along with a monst—er, mother-in-law. All she has to do is show up for the ceremony."

"That's exactly it." Gramma tugs on my hand and motions outside. "Come."

She leads me out front and we settle onto our respective spots on the swing. I give it a little push to start it swaying, then tuck my legs up as I wait for Grams to speak.

"Have you ever heard of your great-aunt Louise?"

I shake my head.

"I didn't figure you had. She and her husband died in a car accident when I was pregnant with your mother."

"I'm...sorry."

"Thank you, sweetie, but that's not why I brought her up. You see, she married straight out of high school and moved to the mainland. She was several years older than me, and I'd never known a life without her. Watching her make plans to go off into the great, wide world and leave the rest of the family behind nearly broke my heart."

"You think that's what's bugging Macie?" I prop my chin

on my knees. "It's not like *I'm* moving to the mainland." At least, I hope not.

"I can't say for sure that's what's bothering her, but I'd her a bit of grace the next time she pulls an attitude with you. She might be struggling more than you know."

"Okay." I stare across the street as the last rays of sunlight wind around the silhouette of a palm tree.

"Anything else on your mind? A certain *monster*-in-law, perhaps?"

"Oh, Grams." I bury my head in my hands, face flaming like a tiki torch. "I didn't mean to say that."

"But you did." Grams brushes salt-and-pepper hair from her eyes. "And though I don't much approve of your word choice, I understand where you're coming from. Midori means well, I'm sure, but she hasn't been the easiest to work with. You handled things very well today."

"Not well enough. What if Brander doesn't want his mom planning the reception? I should've checked with him first, but it all sort of spilled out and then..." I shrug. "I don't feel cut out for this, Grams. If I can't even handle my in-laws, how am I ready to be a wife?"

"No one is ever truly *ready*." Gramma rubs her knobby middle finger against her muumuu-cloaked thigh. "But we all can rise to the occasion." She sits silently a moment and then, as if feeling that she's given me more than enough to chew on for the evening, she climbs slowly to her feet. "Now, I'd better check on Macie."

"How much do I owe you?" The words escape into the encroaching darkness, catching Gramma just before she can step through the door.

"For what?"

"For counseling sessions over the last..." I do a quick

count. "Six years. I must've racked up a pretty big tab by now."

The corners of Gramma's mouth quirk up, creating an avalanche of creases on either side of her nose, and her sapphire-blue eyes—the same ones that got passed down to Mom—twinkle. "Lucky for you, a grandmother's advice is always free for the taking."

And, with that, she disappears inside.

"So." Jazz takes a swig of passionfruit juice and leans against the side of the dilapidated old house-turned-doggie-rescue-mission one lazy afternoon after work. "Any idea what I should get Brander for his birthday?"

"Not a clue." I nudge her prosthesis with my leg, the cool grass tickling my ankle. "*I* couldn't even come up with anything."

"You didn't get him a birthday present?" Jazz's eyes bloom wide across her face. "Olive!"

"Of course I got him something, but you know me. Grams keeps talking about how this is the only birthday we'll celebrate as an engaged couple so I should get him something special. I stink at sappy, sentimental stuff like that."

"Then what'd you get him?"

"Date night in a jar. It was Gramma's idea. I wrapped up a bunch of gift cards to different places and put them in a giant mason jar. He can pick one every month for a year."

"That's so cute." Jazz practically swoons. "I wish someone would make *me* a date night in a jar."

"I bet Hunter would." I waggle my eyebrows at Jazz. "How's he doing on that paperwork?"

"Give me a break." Jazz shoves me so hard I nearly topple over onto the cool grass, and her cheeks turn a telltale shade of pink. "I haven't heard from him since the record thing. I'll give him another day or so before I call. He shouldn't be letting the grass grow under his feet, you know. Especially if he's going to Nashville."

The urge to bug Jazz some more about Hunter is strong, but even stronger is the sharp pain in my gut at the thought of said *record thing.* "Jazz, I do *not* want to move to Nashville."

"Then tell Brander."

"I already did." I cringe. "But then I read this letter from my mom."

I dig the letter out of its near-permanent residence—aka my pocket—and read it aloud. "After I got it, I called Brander to tell him I'd stick with him. Nashville or no Nashville. No matter what. It's only right, you know?" I look to Jazz for confirmation, but her eyes are glazed, like she's totally tuned out. "Is everything okay?"

"Hearing you talk about your mom like that—like she's still here...I don't know." She ducks her head. "Your mom's dead and you two still have, like, this great transcendent bond. My mom lives five minutes away and I only see her if I happen to bump into her at the grocery store. It's not—"

Before Jazz can finish her sentence, a deep howl emanates from the dog kennels across the yard, and Jazz scrambles to her feet. "Guess it's potty time for Goliath. You might want to hide, Olive. This guy's a brute."

I don't need to hear any more. Jazz isn't even halfway across the patchy lawn before I've escaped to relative safety on the deck overlooking the yard. And then, right as Jazz unlocks the kennel and a huge, black-brindled chunk of pit bull rottenness gallops out, something small and tiger-striped streaks across the lawn. "Cat!"

"What?" Jazz hollers as the beast takes off after the feline in question.

"*Cat!*" All of a sudden, I'm six years old again, watching as my kitten, Peaches, is mauled by a canine beast before my very eyes. My leg muscles must forget to check in with my brain though, because suddenly I'm sprinting down the steps and across the yard as the nasty mutt gains on the poor cat.

Closer...closer...

The dog's crooked yellow teeth are nearly close enough to catch the poor kitty's long, feather-duster tail, when I leap. I land on the big, slobbery, ogre with such force that he drops to the ground like the giant he was named after. Lifting my head in the nick of time, I catch a flick of a fluffy tail as the cat—really more of a kitten, judging from the size of it—jumps onto the deck.

*Safe.*

At least, one of us is.

I, however, happen to be sprawled in a heap on top of a growling monster from my very worst nightmares.

"Olive?" Jazz's voice sounds very, very far away.

Goliath shakes me off and climbs to his feet.

I try to cry for help, but the shriek sticks in my throat. This can't be happening right now. *Please, God, let this be a dream.*

The dog towers over me now, mouth wide open, tongue hanging out, teeth bared, and...

He licks me.

*Licks me?*

I scramble to my feet, choking on stench of Goliath's

dog-food breath, and run for cover. I practically collapse on the porch, where the kitten is now grooming his plume of a tail like he didn't almost meet an untimely end. Jazz walks over, lips twitching.

And then I can't take it anymore.

I let out a snort, then a giggle, and Jazz joins in. We laugh until I'm wheezing, gasping for air, and holding my sides. Goliath and the kitten stare at us like we're both nuts.

"Wow, Olive," Jazz gasps between giggles. "You're a hero."

"I couldn't sit there and watch that poor cat get devoured. Who knows what kind of brutality Goliath is capable of?"

"Goliath?" Jazz snickers. "He's ten years old and has gum disease. His teeth would fall out if he tried to eat you."

"Then why did you make it sound like he was so vicious?"

"Because I know you hate pit bulls." Jazz gives Goliath a pat, and he leans his huge, block-like head against her thigh. "I figured you'd rather keep your distance."

"You see how well *that* worked out." I glance at my work shirt, which is now sporting a number of grass stains and a dribble of doggie drool. "What's the deal with the kitten? I thought Dani was dogs-only."

"She is." Jazz lowers herself to the deck, and Goliath instantly flops over with his head in her lap. "This stray's been hanging around for a while though. I think he's hungry. I've been tossing extra puppy kibble out in the lawn for him—that's got to be better than mouse hunting."

"Huh." I sit next to Jazz and click my tongue against the roof of my mouth, the same way Mom taught me to coax over my old kitten. "Here, kitty."

The dark-striped ball of fluff pads cautiously across the porch and sniffs my knee before butting his head up against it, then rolls over onto his back, exposing his—er, *her*—fluffy white belly. "Pretty friendly for a stray."

"Friendly?" Jazz reaches out to pet the cat. The feline instantly ducks and hisses, pressing her ears flat against his head. "That's what he's done every time Dani or I try to get near him."

"Maybe your dog-whispering talents don't translate to cats." I let the kitten sniff my hand before giving her a good scratch behind his fluff-lined ears. She lets out a rumbly purr and stares up at me with eyes so big and blue they almost remind me of Mom's. "You're missing out. This one's a keeper."

Jazz looks on skeptically as the kitten crawls into my lap, curls up in a ball, and promptly falls asleep. "I never thought I'd see the day when Olive Galloway became an animal whisperer." Jazz speaks in a stage whisper, but the laughter in her eyes is louder than the roar of a jet airplane taking off. "You should take him home. He's obviously lonely."

"I wish, but I can't imagine what Zuzu would think of that." Macie's spoiled shih tzu has been an only child—pet?—for years, and something tells me this sweet ball of fluff would start a vicious sibling rivalry.

We fall silent for a moment, Jazz patting Goliath's big, box-shaped head, me stroking the cat's silky ears as she sleeps, until a yell carries around the house from the front porch.

"Anyone home?" The sound of footsteps grows louder, and Hunter rounds the side of the house a few moments later, half his hair scraped into a ponytail, the rest flowing down his neck. And...is that a *braid* in it? I shake my head. Hunter must spend as much time with a hairbrush in the morning as Macie does. I don't get the appeal of the scruffy surfer look myself, but if it's enough to make half a million girls on social media swoon, then there must be *something* to be said for it.

"Hey, Hunter." Jazz pushes Goliath's head from her lap, and it falls to the ground with a mighty thunk. He twitches in his sleep as Jazz hurries to stand, brushing wiry dog hair from her white shorts and tugging at the cuffs. "What's up?"

"I finished." He brandishes a handful of papers. "Figured I'd drop them off before band practice. *If* Brander remembers to show up." Hunter makes a face, like he still isn't over what happened at youth group.

"I'm sure he will." I gently displace the still-sleeping kitten and climb to my feet. "Is Breeze excited about getting a therapy dog?"

"I haven't told her about it yet. It would stink to get her hopes up and have the paperwork not go through. Besides..." he smiles at Jazz. "I'm not in a hurry."

I almost roll my eyes, then stop before Hunter can see me. Seriously though, how much more obvious can a guy get—and how can Jazz be so oblivious?

Unless...

I sneak a peek at Jazz, who raises the paperwork to hide her cheeks, which have turned a pleasant shade of plumeria pink. Maybe...if I could get her to catch my bouquet at the wedding reception...

With Jazz and Hunter still smiling shyly at each other, I reach for my phone and fire off a quick text to Midori: **Where can I get the world's prettiest bouquet?**

After all, if I can manage to rig things so Jazz catches

the bouquet, I'd better make sure it's a bouquet worth catching.

**I know the perfect place. Let's meet soon to discuss.**

Someone must've slipped her a nice pill with her coffee this morning, because there's even a smiling emoji at the end of it the message, like she's actually excited about collaborating on some small aspect of the wedding—about welcoming me into the family.

*Or maybe...* A voice that sounds suspiciously like Mom's whispers in my ear. *Maybe she's been ready to welcome you all along.*

# Chapter Eleven

"HAPPY BIRTHDAY TO YOU, HAPPY BIRTH—"

"Olive!" Brander whirls around in his desk chair when I burst through the door to his office during my lunch break the next day, his face alight despite my painfully off-key singing. "Hey!" He jumps up to give me a long hug, punctuated by a sugar-sweet kiss at the end.

"I brought lunch." I plop two hefty takeout boxes on Brander's desk after he opens his date-in-a-jar gift. The original plan had been to kidnap him and take him on a picnic at the beach, but something tells me that Delacroix Hospitality doesn't do extended lunch breaks. Not even on birthdays. Neither does the *West Maui Sun*, for that matter.

"Awesome." Brander bends in for another kiss and crosses over to lift the lid on the box with his name on it. A massive lobster-avocado sandwich stares up at him, accompanied by a double helping of fries. His cowlick flops in his eyes and he reaches for my hand before bowing his head to pray. "Dear God, thank You for bringing me Olive, and thank You for bringing us together—"

"And thank You for *food*. Amen." I poke Brander in the ribs, and he opens his eyes. "Come on, I'm starving. Let's eat."

We each grab our box and plop on the high-gloss wood floor, backs against the stark white wall, shoulder to shoulder as we dig in. But Brander has barely chewed through his first mouthful when the phone on his desk lets out a shrill, whiny ring.

Brander closes his eyes for a moment, as if praying for wisdom, before opening his mouth and taking another bite.

"You can take that. I don't mind." If I was a certain wooden puppet, my nose would be stretching all the way across the room at that statement, but I take a deep breath and reach for the words from Mom's letter. *Every part of him. I want every part.*

Even a job that is, in my opinion, way too much work with nowhere near enough reward. Thankfully, Brander doesn't so much as blink at the phone. "I'm on my lunch break—and it's my birthday. They can leave a message."

And so they do, begging Brander to call them ASAP. He listens carefully, then takes another bite of sandwich. "Mom said you invited her over for lunch." He arches his brow, turning a casual statement into a loaded question.

"I need help picking out a bouquet. I figure she knows more florists on the island than anyone else in town. I—I'm trying to set up Jazz and Hunter."

"Hunter and Jazz? For real?"

"Dead serious. Keep an eye on them the next time we all hang out together and tell me if there isn't something there. I'm going to try and rig it so Jazz catches my bouquet at the reception, but I want the bouquet to be *perfect*. I figure your mom knows more about perfection than most people."

"That's for sure." He leans into me, face growing serious. "For real though, thanks for making an effort with her. I know she can be a little tough to deal with sometimes, but she means well. Honest."

"I know. Besides, when I said yes to your proposal, it didn't end that night—it means I'm still saying yes. To your parents, your crazy job...and your music." Those last words are softer, more hesitant. "I meant what I said on Saturday. Nashville or no Nashville, I'm with you all the way."

Brander stares at me, eyes wide. He blinks once. Then again. And then...

"No, don't cry. I didn't mean anything by it. I was only saying—"

"I know what you were saying." Brander lays his takeout box on the ground and wraps his arms around me. "You're willing to give up everything for me."

"Everything? Nah. You'll never get me to part with my Jane Austen."

Brander pulls me closer. "But when it matters, I know you're with me. And I haven't been doing that for you. I'm so busy with work and—"

"Hello?" A door slams against the wall, and high heels click against the shiny wood floor. "Mr. Dela—*oh.*" The woman's voice is one note shy of scandalized, and my cheeks flame as Brander hurriedly disentangles himself and climbs to his feet.

"Hi, Kathi." His voice is smooth and easy, like he didn't just get caught eating takeout—and hugging his fiancée—on his office floor. "What's up?"

"If you were in here all this time, then why didn't you answer the call from the New Mexico Orthopedic Association? I put their call through to you a moment ago."

"I'm on my lunch break." He almost mumbles the words, like he's a kid caught with his hand in the cookie jar and shuffles his shiny work shoes. "I figured they would leave a message if it was important."

"And did they?" For a receptionist, this lady's got a lot of nerve. It's all I can do to keep from climbing to my feet and very nicely informing her that she can go pound sand, so instead I keep my mouth occupied with my lobster roll while Kathi rambles on and on about nothing long enough to prove her point.

By the time she finishes her pseudo-lecture, the sparkle has gone off our lunch break, and it's time for me to leave. Brander and I share a pained, strained glance that says more than words ever could, and his kiss goodbye is bitter-sweet. It would be one thing if we could go out for a make-up dinner tonight, but Brander's leading worship for youth group again.

That is, if he makes it out of work alive.

"It's bad, Jazz. Really bad." I flop into a seat next to Jazz as soon as I get to youth group. Macie—technically still too young for youth group but stubbornly determined to make her presence known—is at her side.

"What's bad?" Macie stares across the pavilion to where Gramma is helping several volunteers lay out supplies for make-your-own kalua pork sandwiches.

"Brander's job. He has a dictator for a receptionist, and his phone is ringing off the hook."

"Then why does he work there?" Macie snaps her gum and twists a piece of half-straightened hair around her finger as she leans back in her chair. "I liked him better when he worked at the Shave Ice Shack anyway. He was less stuffy then."

Jazz nods. "I don't fault him for working for his parents, but he's awfully busy. Hunter's afraid he'll bail on the whole band thing before they can even consider the record deal." Jazz pushes Macie's hands away from her frizzing mass of hair and gathers it in three sections to twine into a braid.

"Talking to Hunter again?" I waggle my eyebrows, but Jazz silences me with a look and a quick gesture to where Hunter's sitting, nearly within earshot. "Whatever. I agree. The Nashville thing is starting to sound like the lesser of two evils. I had no idea the corporate world was so intense."

"You guys are getting boring, you know it?" Macie pops her gum again. "All you ever talk about is dumb grown-up stuff. Remember when you used to go paddleboarding and sleep out on the porch and actually have *fun*?"

Macie's words hit a little closer to home than I'd like—especially on a day like today, when Brander's birthday surprise was effectively ruined by said dumb grown-up stuff.

"She's got a point." Jazz pokes me as Brander and Hunter take the stage to start the worship set. "Why don't we do something fun this weekend—just us girls?"

Macie instantly brightens and gives her gum an extra-loud crack. "Could we go out for shave ice?"

"I was thinking more like a spa day—do each other's nails, try out different hairstyles for the wedding, all that."

"That sounds like fun." A bubble of pleasure rises in my chest, even though I'm not normally the mani-pedi type. Maybe Midori is rubbing off on me. The thought nearly makes me giggle, but the laughter dies in my throat at the sour look on Macie's face.

"No thanks." She knots her arms tightly over her chest and frowns. "I'm kind of over the whole wedding thing."

"Macie!" My little sister's words cut deep, and I can't help raising my voice. Thankfully, before our famous Galloway tempers can get us roped into a verbal sparring match, Brander strums a chord and the crowd grows quiet.

But even though Brander's indie-pop rendition of "Way Maker" gets me and Jazz on our feet, Macie stays slumped in her chair like someone has her tied there. Her eyes are filled with fire, her lips stretched thin across her face.

"What's wrong?" I bend to whisper to her in between songs, but she shrugs me off.

"Leave me alone." Macie's eyes turn wide and glassy, a sudden wetness extinguishing the blazing spark they held before. She bows her head over her tightly clasped hands.

My heart twinges. Whatever's hurting her hurts me too—even if I have no idea what that is.

*Or maybe I do.*

An improvised guitar riff drifts through the air, and beyond the pavilion, clouds billow around the horizon with a sort of urgency that signifies a storm on its way. A shiver starts down my spine, but then I feel it—a little tickle in my mind, echoing the words that Gramma spoke not so long ago.

*Watching her make plans to go off into the great, wide world and leave the rest of the family behind nearly broke my heart.*

As Brander and Hunter start their next song, I find myself praying more than singing. By the end of the worship set, I know exactly what I need to do.

# Chapter Twelve

"HEY, MACE, I'M KIDNAPPING YOU." I meet Macie as she bounds down the steps from her school to the parking lot on Friday afternoon and wrap a silky white scarf—borrowed from Jazz's old stash—around her eyes.

"Kidnapping me?" Macie squeaks as I tie the makeshift blindfold a little too tight. "Okay! Bye guys!" With a general wave in the direction of her friends, she lets me pull her through the parking lot and into my waiting car.

"Buckle up and hang on. We're going on an adventure." I crack the sunroof, and the sweet smell of plumeria fills the space between us as we pull out of the parking lot. "How was school?"

"Fine. What kind of an adventure?" Macie bounces a little in her seat—like she used to when she was little—and slips off her blindfold. "Is there going to be food? I'm starving."

"Just you wait, squirt." The old nickname still comes easily, even though Macie technically *isn't* a squirt anymore. She's almost as tall as I am—though that's not saying much.

Before I can turn into a sentimental sap over the fact that my little sister isn't a shrimpy elementary schooler anymore, I flip on the radio and get Macie in on an epic lip-sync battle that lasts until we reach our destination.

"Put that blindfold back on." I pretend to give her the stink eye as I pull into a parking space in front of the bakery I found online. Turns out Brander's mom doesn't have much of a sweet tooth, and we decided that this is one wedding-planning duty I can take care of...with a little help from the pastry queen herself. "Ready for a snack?"

"When am I not?" Blindfold secure, Macie bounces out of the car like a beach ball and nearly trips over a crack in the sidewalk.

"Careful, Mace." I hold her by the elbow as we make our way up the front walk—right on time.

When we reach the entrance, I unfasten Macie's blindfold, leaving the scarf to drape around her neck. Before Macie can badger me with any more questions, I push open the heavy double doors leading to the Mona Mona Bakery.

Instantly, I'm hit in the face with a burst of warm, sugar-scented air. Macie practically starts drooling as we survey the large, white showroom, crammed full of a variety of confections ranging from simple sheet cakes to epic, twelve-tier masterpieces.

"I'm working here when I grow up." Macie's words are soft and almost reverent, but they must catch the ear of a middle-aged woman standing behind an icing-smudged counter at one end of the room, because she glances up and smiles.

"Aloha, ladies. Are you here for a tasting?"

Macie claps one hand over her mouth when I nod, and she grips my hand tightly as we walk over to the woman.

"Olive? I'm Valentina." Her voice is lightly brushed with an accent I can't quite place—French, maybe—and she lays aside an insanely real-looking frosting flower to scribble on a powdered-sugar-dusted clipboard. "Mahalo for considering us to provide the goodies for your special day. If you'll follow me, I have the tasting room all ready for you."

Macie's spine stiffens a little at the words *special day,*

but the promise of a cake-tasting session at a pro bakery like this must be enough to mollify her, because she prances after me and Valentina into a small room overlooking a grove of plumeria trees.

I turn toward Macie as she clasps her hands to her chest and stares, slack-jawed, at a table lined with more pieces of cake than a person could eat in a lifetime. ""Is all of this for *us*?" Olive, you didn't kidnap me. You took me to Heaven."

Valentina muffles a chuckle with one hand and hands me the clipboard she's been writing on. "You'll notice that each cake plate has a number. Here's a list with numbers, flavors, and prices. You can make notes on it if you so choose, to help you keep your favorites straight. I have some more icing roses to make, but feel free to take your time. I'll check in later."

With that, the door slams shut with a click and retreating footsteps echo in the hall.

"I'm locked in a room with twenty different kinds of cake." Macie shakes her head like she can't believe it, then grabs a plate and shovels a huge forkful into her mouth. Her eyes roll back in her head, and for a moment it legitimately looks like she might faint. She doesn't, though—just collapses into a cushy white armchair and holds the cake plate aloft like it's a precious treasure. "Olive, you have *got* to taste this."

I plop onto the chair next to her, and Macie pops a forkful of cake right in my mouth. Instantly I'm hit with the creamy richness of cream cheese frosting and the moist, pecan-studded spiciness of carrot cake. "Yum."

"*Yum?* All you can say is *yum?*" Macie goes on, prattling about crumb density and sifting baking powder and a bunch of things I have no knowledge of until she finally runs out of breath. "What I'm saying, Olive, is that this is the best carrot cake I've ever had in my *life*. It has to be the one."

"Not so fast, Mace. There are still nineteen more to go."

I tap out after my tenth taste, but Macie keeps going, chomping her way through all twenty different varieties until she can offer her expert opinion. "It's got to be carrot cake. Or the honey-lavender. Or lemon-coconut. They're all so amazing though, I can't choose." She wipes her mouth on an embossed white napkin and stares out the window. When she speaks again, her tone is different—almost somber. "Olive?"

"Yeah?"

"Why did you pick me to come with you? I mean, Brander's the one who's going to be stuffing cake in your face at the wedding. Shouldn't he have been here?"

"He'll stop by later to help us make the final decision. But..." I scoot my chair closer to Macie's, clear my throat, and prepare to deliver the little speech I planned out in bed late last night. "I wanted to do the first tasting with you, Mace. You're my baker extraordinaire. Why wouldn't I want your opinion?"

Macie squints at me, like my words can't possibly be true. "Gramma's a better baker than I am."

"But Gramma's not my sister." I poke her in the side. "*You* are. You're one of my best friends too. And..." The rest of the words of my speech die on my tongue, and I reach into my pocket to pull out the necklace Grams helped me make yesterday. "This is for you. I want you to wear it when you stand up with me at my wedding."

"Whoa." Macie takes the delicate silver chain and holds it up, two heart-shaped sea-glass pendants twinkling in the sunlight streaming in through the window. It had been a while since I'd done an art project, and it felt good to craft with Gramma again. Now, seeing the awed look on Macie's face, it feels even better. "Did Gram make this?"

"We both did, after you went to bed."

One corner of Macie's mouth quirks up. "What did you mean about me standing up with you at the wedding? I'm too old to be a flower girl."

"Yeah, but you're never too old—or too young—to be a bridesmaid."

Macie's eyes fly wide open and she jumps out of her chair, clutching the necklace to her chest and flinging herself at me in a hug. "You mean it? I get to wear a fancy dress and fancy shoes and—oh!—do you think Grams will let me wear makeup?"

"I don't know." I return Macie's hug before helping her fasten the necklace. "But I can guarantee you'll get the fancy dress and the shoes. I checked with the bridal boutique, and they have a junior bridesmaid dress with all kinds of blue ombre layers."

"Like the one I had you try on?" Macie does a little dance right there in the tasting room right as the door opens and Valentina ushers Brander inside.

"What's the verdict?" Valentina's voice is soft and professional, like junior-bridesmaids-to-be do victory dances in her tasting room every afternoon.

"They're amazing. Did you make all of these? I literally can't stop eating any of them." Macie takes another bite of carrot cake right then and there to prove it, and I'm half-surprised she doesn't ask for the lady's autograph. "We have it down to three, though. Brander can make the final call." Macie hands over the clipboard.

"Wonderful then. I'll bring in fresh slices of each."

Valentina disappears and reappears almost instantly, expertly juggling three plates bearing fresh slices of cake. Brander settles into an armchair next to the table.

"How are you?" I hand him the first plate of cake.

He offers a half-smile in response. "Tired. Ready for cake." He must've had a lot of important meetings today, because his cowlick is bowed in submission under the weight of what must be half a bottle of hair gel. He's also wearing a dreadfully stiff necktie that is no doubt Midori's doing. "You say *I'm* making the call, huh?" His brow pinches, like he's intimidated by such a great challenge, but he dutifully taste-tests all three flavors.

"Well? What do you think?" Macie bounces in her chair, fingers twined around her new necklace, expectancy painted over every freckle on her face.

"I like the carrot cake, but..."

"It's not really right for a wedding, is it? Rats." Macie snaps her fingers. "It was my favorite. What about the other two?"

Brander takes another bite of each. "I think we should go with...both."

"Both?" Macie and I speak at the same time, and Macie giggles. "How would that work?" she asks.

"Easy." Brander pulls out his phone. After a few quick taps, he shows us a photo of a cake with four different tiers, each one with a varying decorative style. "This was my cousin's wedding cake. He's a chocoholic, but his wife's favorite flavor is vanilla. Eventually they decided to make each tier a different flavor. It was awesome."

"Perfect. Problem solved." Macie claps her hands and checks both boxes on the cake order form. "Maybe this wedding-planning business isn't so bad after all."

I take in a deep breath of sugar-scented air and share a smile with Brander as Macie sneaks a final bite of carrot cake. *Problem solved indeed.*

But later that night, as Macie, Brander, and I join Grams around the dinner table, I catch Macie staring at my engagement ring, the corners of her mouth quivering in an almost-frown. We're growing up—both of us.

Does that mean we're destined to grow apart?

# Chapter Thirteen

"GOOD AFTERNOON, OLIVIA." MIDORI GIVES A slight bow and kicks off her slingback shoes when I open the door to greet her one Saturday afternoon, and I can't help but cringe.

Mom was only one person on earth who could ever get away with calling me Olivia—the name I was supposed to have had in the first place. Even then, it was only as a joke. Now that she's gone...my heart pinches. I'd give anything to correct Midori, but she seems genuinely excited about helping me pick out a bouquet. I'd like to keep it that way. "Good afternoon."

I hold the door open wider and she sweeps through it, juggling an overstuffed binder and several glossy, double-issue bridal magazines. "You look lovely today."

"Thanks. Would you like some lemonade?" My voice sounds a little stiff as I lead her into the dining room, almost like I'm nervous. And let's face it—I kind of am. Grams has an afternoon shift at the gallery, and Macie took Zuzu over to Jazz's for a puppy playdate, which means it's me and Midori. Alone.

Maybe I should've invited Brander to come too. Maybe he'd know the right words to use to stand up to his mom. Maybe...*forget it.*

I can't expect Brander to be my security blanket every time I'm around his mother. One way or another, Midori and I have to build a relationship of our own.

We make small talk over a takeout meal of dumplings

and wontons from Lahaina's favorite pan-Asian joint, Star Noodle, Midori nodding in silent approval at my use of chopsticks, until I reach over to grab her binder. "Looks like you brought way more than a few florist suggestions. What all's in here?"

"Ideas." Midori lays her chopsticks aside with a slight clatter and whisks the binder out of my hands before I can even riffle through the pages. "And surprises. Not for you to see."

"Oops." I duck my head. "Sorry."

"No harm done." Midori carefully opens the binder and flips through the pages to a spread featuring enough bridal bouquets to give anyone with allergies an instant sneezing fit. "Ah, here we go. These are all examples from some of the island's most reputable florists."

She points to each option, rattling off pricing and options for coordinating boutonnières, but her voice fades into the background as I'm met with the dizzying array of photographs. In classic Midori form, most of the bouquets are way over-the-top—but not necessarily in a bad way. Especially since this bouquet is just as much for Jazz as it is me.

I scan the page, skipping over the gaudier bouquets—definitely too elaborate for the bohemian ceremony in my mind's eye—until a photograph of a cascading, almost wild-looking collection of flowers and fronds catches my eye. Not only is the bouquet filled with some of my favorite tropical flowers, but it's also trimmed with seagrass and cascading greens and a bunch of stuff I never expected to see in a wedding bouquet. It sort of reminds me of...

*Mom.*

Almost without thinking, I pull the picture of Mom on her wedding day—the one from her letter—out of my pocket and slide it across the table to Midori. "This was my mom's bouquet." I tap the photo, then the picture on Midori's collage that caught my eye. "It reminds me of this one."

"Hmm." Midori ducks her head and examines first one picture, then the other, before sliding Mom's photograph back to me. "You look alike."

My breath catches in my throat. "We do?"

"Haven't you looked in a mirror before? Your faces are identical."

"Minus the blue eyes." I point to my own, which got the unfortunate color of a murky green swamp. "But thanks. That means a lot."

"You miss her?" Midori fingers a strand of silk-smooth hair before tucking it behind her ear.

"So much." My throat grows warm and prickly. "Especially now. She would've flipped over the chance to help me plan a wedding."

Midori's expression morphs into something I've never seen from her before. A sort of kindness warms her eyes, and something—sympathy?—plumps the corners of her mouth in a half-smile. "Losing a parent is terrible." Even her voice is soft, almost hesitant. "My father died when I was very young."

"Oh." A lump fills my throat, and I picture Midori as a toddler, growing up without a dad. And then as a girl about my age, getting married. "Who walked you down the aisle then?" If there could be anything as bad as not having Mom sitting in the front pew, it would be not having Dad there to give me away.

"My mother did." Midori lifts her chin. "She was the bravest woman I ever knew. We came here from Japan when we had nothing. She started off as a maid at the Ka'anapali

Beach Hotel and worked up to a management position."

"Is she how you got into the resort business?"

"Yes. And she introduced me to Auggie."

"Does she still live in Lahaina?"

"No." Midori dips her head and fans the pages of her binder once, then twice, then again. "She is...no longer with us."

"You mean—"

"Her body is still here, but her mind...she has dementia." Midori blinks hard and fast for a few seconds, like she might cry. Her expression is hollow—like her heart has taken off to join her mother in a hidden dimension somewhere between the present and the past. "About this bouquet. You should order it as soon as possible. And you'll need to have your wedding colors picked out before you do, so you can make any special requests."

"Okay." I tap a finger alongside the photo of Mom. "I want all cream. Maybe a little blush, like in Mom's bouquet. And lots of greenery."

Midori jots down half a page of notes. "Blush or peach? There's a difference, you know."

"There is?"

"Blush is pinker. Peach is more natural."

"Uh, peach then." And then, glancing at the photo once more, I'm seized by a sudden boldness. "Midori, what about your mom—will she be at the wedding?"

"As I said, she is no longer with us. Shall we discuss the boutonnières?" Midori snaps her mouth shut, stamping a giant *case closed* sign across her face for all the world to see. A warning not to dig too deep.

The only problem—I've never been good at heeding warnings.

"One last thing before I leave." Midori stands halfway out the door, shifting her weight from one foot to the other. "I've been waiting for the best time to bring this up, but perhaps Jazmine would take this better if you spoke with her about it first."

"Take what better?" Midori should know Jazz well enough by now to know that she's not the kind of girl to *take* anything.

Midori squares her shoulders. "I'd like to buy her a second leg."

"A...what?"

"A leg. A cosmetic one."

"Why, may I ask, would Jazz need a cosmetic leg?"

"I thought it would be nice for her to have, so she can look—"

"Look what? *Normal?* Jazz's prosthesis is her normal. Are you afraid all that shiny metal isn't going to fit with your decor?"

"Not the decor, no..." The binder slips from Midori's arm, and she reaches out a trembling hand to steady it. "August and I discussed it. We felt that she might feel more comfortable with a, well, a normal leg. For pictures and things."

"Jazz's leg isn't designer enough for you? It's not supposed to be. It's a leg—same as one of mine." Try as I might, I can't disguise my huff. "I'm sorry, but even if Jazz and Macie and Gramma and I aren't picture-perfect, you're going to have to deal with it. We're *ohana,* and family doesn't give up on family." I stand with my arms crossed over my chest and wait for her to fire back.

She doesn't.

Instead, Midori lowers her head, blinks slowly a few times, and inches out the front door without another word. I open my mouth to apologize, but Midori has already slipped on her shoes and clack-clacked down the driveway to her car before I can come up with the words.

I run after her, but by the time I reach the curb, she's already fired up her white Ferrari and peeled away in a cloud of exhaust.

Game over.

The score? "Olivia" Galloway and Midori Delacroix—tied at negative one.

# Chapter Fourteen

"WE NEED TO TALK." I BELLOW the words like an angry hippopotamus and slam the door behind me as I march into the living room of Dani's dog rescue place. "You won't *believe* what that woman said I should—um, hi."

I round the corner to find not only Jazz and Macie but also Hunter and a girl around Macie's age who shares his trademark mess of tawny curls. They're all sprawled on the floor along with half a dozen dogs. Jazz, Macie, and Hunter all look at each other, practically with question marks dancing around their heads, but the other girl only stares. "You must be Breeze." I kneel in front of her and offer my hand to shake, but she stares right through me—into me?

"You were very loud." Her voice is flat. Her eyes bore a hole through me like I'm a flimsy piece of driftwood.

My cheeks heat. "Sorry about that. I didn't scare you, did I?"

"No. But you startled Mango."

"Mango?"

"She does not like loud people." Breeze stares at the cat—the same one I rescued from that pit bull—that's purring in her lap.

My fingers itch to reach out and pat the kitten's fluffy coat, but she's sleeping soundly in Breeze's lap. I hate to disturb either of them. "Looks like she likes you."

"She does. I like cats." Breeze ducks her head and plunges her fingers into the kitten's striped fur.

"Dani decided to adopt her?" I turn my gaze on Jazz, the anger boiling in my chest relaxing into a healthy simmer.

Jazz shakes her head. "Breeze was holding her when I answered the door. Guess you're not the only cat charmer on the island."

"Huh." Something strange sparks in my chest. Not jealousy, exactly, but a strange sort of possessiveness. Maybe Zuzu wouldn't mind so much if...

"Is everything okay?" Jazz leans in closer and drops her voice. "You're glaring at that poor cat like it has rabies."

"I am?"

Jazz nods.

"Yeah, I probably am. Can you talk?"

"Hunter and Breeze have only been here for a few minutes. I can't kick them out now."

All I want to do is grab Jazz, drag her outside, and unload everything that's gone on in the past hour or so, but I know very well that I can't expect her to be my crisis counselor when she's supposed to be working. Instead, I paste a smile on my face. "Fine." It must come out more like a growl than I'd intended, because Jazz shoots me the stink eye. "I mean, sure. Take your time."

Something tells me my second attempt wasn't much better than my first, but I doubt Jazz would blame me if she knew the reason behind my attitude.

She'll know soon enough, anyhow.

Finally, Hunter and his sister leave, Breeze giving that cat a hug goodbye and clinging so desperately to it that I'm afraid she'll smother the poor thing. Mango must be some cat to be willing to put up with that much affection.

Macie barely waits three seconds after the door closes behind them before snorting. "Hunter seriously wants you to believe that Breeze wants a *dog*?"

Jazz turns to Macie with wide, innocent eyes. "What do you mean?"

"It's obvious Breeze is way more into cats. Or stuffed animals. Why is Hunter wasting his time over here? Unless—"

"Macie!" Jazz's voice creeps up to an almost-yelp. "Why don't you take the puppies outside and work on toilet training?"

Macie's face falls. "But—"

"I do *not* want to have to clean up another accident in here." Jazz points to the front door. "Out."

"Whatever." Macie tucks one puppy under each arm, whistling for Zuzu to follow. "Come on, Zuzu. Let's show them how it's done."

This time, it's Jazz who can barely wait until the front door swings shut. She turns on me the second Macie's footsteps pound down the porch steps. "What on the valley isle were you *doing* when you came in here? You could've scared the dogs—or Breeze. This'd better be good."

I scoop the cat into my arms, careful not to squeeze her quite as tightly as Breeze did, and stare at the feline's fluffy face. Somehow, something in the cat's calm, cool gaze makes me feel a little bit closer to Mom. "Midori wants to buy you another leg." For all of the anger bubbling in my chest, it comes out quiet and calm. *Huh.*

"She...wait, what? Why?"

I tell her everything about the cosmetic leg and how, Midori is presumably terrified at the thought of Jazz's bionic piece of plastic and steel ruining her wedding aesthetic. "Can you believe her? After lunch I'd actually started to think that she could be *nice*, but—"

"Wait a minute." Jazz's voice is soft and slow. The

irritation and offense I'd expected to find on her face is strangely missing. "She wants to get me another prosthesis—like, one that doesn't make me look like a cyborg?"

"It's the shallowest, most inconsiderate thing I've ever heard of. And she was too chicken to even ask you about it herself. I—I'm sorry, Jazz. I should've told her no myself."

"Are you kidding me?" Jazz practically leaps off the floor, startling the poor kitten right out of my arms. "Those things are like five thousand bucks."

"Figures." It goes to show how much money Midori is willing to dump on a hunk of plastic in order to ensure that her picture-perfect party goes as planned.

"What do you mean? I don't get what the big deal is—except that she's *buying me a leg*."

"She wants to change you."

"No. She wants to *improve* me." Jazz picks at her prosthesis liner. "You've got to admit, this thing isn't very attractive."

"But it's *you*."

"Yeah..." Jazz flips her braid over one shoulder and tugs on the tail. "But what if I had ugly crooked teeth instead?"

"Huh?"

"If I had ugly teeth and Midori wanted me to get braces, would you be mad?"

I chew on my lower lip for a second as birdsong floats in through an open window. "I guess not. I mean, that would be a nice offer. Braces are expensive and—"

"Exactly. So are cosmetic legs. And..." her voice drops. "I've wanted one for a long time."

"You *have*?"

"Robot-style limbs aren't exactly on trend."

"You're not offended?"

"Do I look like it?" Jazz beams at me.

"No."

"Trust me. I'm anything but upset." She stares at her leg again, then looks up at me. "Why are *you* so bent out of shape over it?"

"Because Midori doesn't even care about people—about you. And she has a mom stuck in a dementia ward somewhere that she's not even going to invite to the wedding."

"She said all that?"

"Not exactly. But I might've accused her of being a heartless control freak. Not in so many words, thank goodness." Even still, I can feel my cheeks flushing tiki-torch red. "How am I going to get myself out of this one?"

"My mom's been hiding out in her bedroom all afternoon." Brander's gaze is heavy as he turns to me after the waitress at Fleetwood's takes our orders later that afternoon. "And something tells me she isn't busy making wedding plans. Did lunch go okay?"

My throat clogs with a million different words—apologies, explanations, the works—but the only ones that seem to fit are simple. "I was wrong."

"You? Wrong?" Brander's face lights, and I'd accuse him of laughing at me if I wasn't already snickering.

"Really wrong." I tell him about the cosmetic leg, how I was so sure Jazz would balk at Midori's offer that I didn't even give her a chance. "I said some...*stuff*."

"Yikes." Brander tips his glass back and takes a long, long drink of water. "What did *she* say?"

"Nothing. She just left."

"She didn't say *anything*?" Brander bites his lip. "That's

not like her."

"She must be mad then."

Brander shakes his head. "When Mom gets mad, the whole world knows it. Unless all of those self-help books are finally starting to pay off."

"They must be. *I* sure wouldn't have stayed quiet over what I said."

"Maybe this'll be easier if you tell me exactly what happened." Brander leans in close. "Whatever it is, I'm sure we can work it out."

I take a deep breath of air, tinged as much with relief as it is the scent of frying fish. "I didn't come right out and say it, but I kind of made it sound like she's too self-absorbed. Like she doesn't care about her family."

"What?" Brander's eyebrows jump halfway up his head, but the waitress swoops in with two plates loaded with Korean-style chicken sandwiches and fries before he can say anything more. He keeps his eyes fixed on mine until she's out of earshot, then leans in close. "Olive, my mom loves her family more than life itself."

"Then why doesn't she want her own mother at our wedding? I don't care if she has dementia or not. She should be there."

"*Obaasan* has her good days, but on her bad...well, she says a lot of stuff that she shouldn't. Mom and I figured you wouldn't want to chance that at the wedding."

"Wait a minute." I drop my gaze from Brander to my chicken sandwich, which suddenly look way less appetizing than it did a few moments before. "You said *we.*"

Brander reaches across the table for my hand. "Mom and I talked about it after I proposed. She wants so badly for our day to be perfect, and she's afraid Grandma will mess that up if she comes. We both decided—"

"Stop right there." A lump rises in my chest, and suddenly all I want is to run to Midori, wrap my arms around her, and give her a hug—not the same kind of timid embrace she gives me, but the kind of hug I'd give Jazz or Gramma or Macie. "You two shouldn't make big decisions like that without me, for one. For two..."

I take a deep breath, my own words about *ohana* from earlier stirring in my chest. "Your grandma is family, and family doesn't give up on family. Even if they're embarrassing. Come on." I toss my napkin on the table and start across the restaurant rooftop, ready to find our waitress and ask for a box. It's been too long already—I owe Midori the apology she deserves.

"Olive." There's a tug at my hand, and I turn to find Brander smiling at me. "Don't run away."

My lips quirk up sheepishly. "Sorry. But what if it's been too long? What if your mom won't forgive me?"

"She will. *Later.* Come on—let's eat." He draws me back to the table and drops a kiss on my cheek as I slide into my seat, letting his hands rest on my own for a moment as he offers up a prayer.

But even as he asks a quick blessing over our food, I find my heart whispering different words. *God, forgive me. Help me love Midori the way I should—the way You'd want me to. Amen.*

*Oh, and Lord? You'd better help her to be willing to forgive me, too.*

# Chapter Fifteen

DESPITE MY BEST INTENTIONS, IT'S NEARLY midnight by the time we finally finish our dinner—too late to head home with Brander and apologize right then and there without risking surprising a pajamaed-and-mud-masked Midori. Instead, I order a to-go slice of Fleetwood's cream cheese-iced banana bread cake and write a quick note:

*Midori, I'm sorry for what I said today. I'd like to make it up to you somehow, and I'd love to meet your mom. Text me so we can set something up. P.S. Jazz is super excited about the leg!*

I scribble a heart, then sign my name before slipping the piece of paper into a corner of the takeout box. "Make sure your mom eats that cake, okay? That much sugar and cream cheese is enough to cheer anyone up."

"Will do." Brander gives me a mock salute, cake box in hand.

By the time I pull into the driveway at home, my phone is loaded with new messages. There are three voicemails from various scammers, a message from Brander—a clandestine snapshot of his mom chowing down on the cake, a half-smile on her face—and a text from the mom in question.

**Please don't feel obligated to apologize. We were both out of line.**

**Yeah, but** ... I bite my lip and stare at the phone. **I was out-of-line-er.**

A couple of seconds pass, and I shift in my car seat,

cringing at the use of the made-up word. Oh, well. What can Midori expect from a brain-addled bridezilla at almost-midnight? I should've gone over anyway.

But, since my pajamas are currently calling my name, I tap on the phone icon instead. Maybe it would be easier to call.

And then...

A ping announces the arrival of a laughing face emoji. From Midori. I nearly drop the phone.

Three dancing dots show that she's still typing, and I let the phone screen fall dark as I wait for her text to come through. Finally, it does.

Looks like I'm going on a field trip.

Midori's hands grip tighter and tighter around her suede leather steering wheel as we near the Kahului city limits. Thanks to crazy work schedules and Midori's packed social calendar, it's been weeks since I first suggested the trip. But, if Midori's clenched jaw and pale cheeks are anything to go by, I have a feeling she'd put the trip off forever if she could.

By the time we pull into the parking lot at the memory care center, Midori's face is whiter than the inside of a coconut. Her hands tremble as she unbuckles her seatbelt and unfolds herself from the car.

We follow Midori into the care center's lobby and down the hall to a small, dimly lit room. He reaches for my hand as we step inside, and I cling tightly to it as I focus through the darkness on a wheelchair holding a small, shriveled woman. "It's been a while since we've visited." Brander keeps his voice low. "I doubt *Obaasan* will remember us."

As if she hears us and is determined to prove us wrong,

Brander's grandmother snaps to attention the second her daughter flicks on the light. "Midori!" She gasps, eyes filling with sudden tears, and rattles off a string of half-halting words in Japanese.

Brander leans low, his breath tickling my ear. "She might not remember how to speak English today." He releases my hand and steps forward, dipping into a strange little half-bow before his grandma. *"Kon'nichiwa Obaasan."*

"You speak Japanese?"

"Only a little." He motions for me to step forward. *"Obaasan* this is my fiancée, Olive."

"Fiancée." Brander's grandma drops her head and repeats the word to herself over and over, her tongue moving clumsily over the syllables, before she finally focuses on me. *"Kon'nichiwa."*

I repeat the Japanese greeting, my own tongue suddenly clumsy, and bend over in the same sort of bowing motion Brander made earlier. "It's nice to meet you."

The woman's eyes narrow, and I get the feeling that I'm being scrutinized within an inch of my life. "But I like you. You sing too?"

I shake my head.

"Brander is very good."

"I know." I lay my hand over the old woman's. "It's one of the reasons I love him so much."

"I am pleased to meet you, Olive." Brander's grandma keeps her head raised, but her eyes wander around the room, as if she's suddenly lost. "You will be good for our family. My husband will be happy to meet you. He'll be along..." Her fingers fumble with the lap belt on her wheelchair, as if she's preparing to stand, but Midori is too fast for her.

She swoops in and plants her hands on *Obaasan*'s shoulders. "Don't be ridiculous, Mother. Dad has been dead for over forty years."

"Dead?" *Obaasan*'s eyes fill with tears. Her lip quivers. "Why didn't anyone tell me?"

"Mother…" Something in Midori's face breaks—but only for a second. Then the steely mask reappears. "Don't you remember?"

"Remember what? You never tell me anything!" *Obaasan*'s voice creeps up to a wail, and she covers her face, hands shaking. When she speaks again, it's in a torrent of Japanese, the words raining down on us like bullets, each one lodging in my heart.

What must it be like for Midori, standing right next to her mom yet an entire universe apart? As hard as it was saying goodbye to Mom so early, she at least kept her mind until the end. Maybe, in a way, that made it easier.

As if drawn by invisible strings, I slip across the cramped room and rest my hand over Midori's. "It's going to be okay."

"No." Midori extricates her hand from mine and backs away, crossing her arms tightly over her chest. "As long as my mother is trapped between worlds, things will never be right."

"I want her at my wedding." The words march out of my mouth like little soldiers in a line as the three of us sit outside with *Obaasan* later that afternoon.

"No." Midori shakes her head, her eyes landing on *Obaasan*'s open, gaping—and toothless—mouth. The old woman lets out a loud snore. "Look at her."

My heart gives a kick, and it's as if someone turned a burner on to start my blood boiling. "I see her. And I love her."

"But she's—"

"Not perfect? Neither am I." I clamp my mouth shut to keep more words from coming out until I'm sure I've found the right ones. "When I said yes to Brander, I said yes to *all of him*. His family, too. I want *Obaasan* at my wedding."

At that, Midori lets out a small squeak. Two twin tears spill from her eyes. She presses her pale, dainty hands to her face, and her shoulders shake silently. "It won't be what I'd dreamed. She—she might not even understand who's getting married."

"Mom, it's okay." Brander presses into Midori on one side, and I wrap my arm around her from the other. "When our dreams don't come true, that means God has something better planned."

"Better?" Midori's voice is jagged. Broken. She sounds more like a person—a *friend*—than the monster-in-law I'd made her out to be. "How could *this* be better?"

"I don't understand it." I tighten my hold on Midori. "But I know Someone who does."

Midori's spine stiffens. "If He really knows our hearts and understands how hard it is to watch her struggle, then how can He allow this suffering to continue?"

"Mom." Brander slips from his seat and kneels on the cobblestone patio in front of Midori. Gently, tenderly, he takes her hands and lifts his eyes to meet her own. "I don't get why God lets things happen the way He does, but I do know that He always has a plan. Even when we can't see it. Even when it hurts."

At that, *Obaasan* stirs in her wheelchair. Her eyes slowly

open, dark brown pupils glimmering like beads amid a tapestry of crow's feet. She lifts her head and peers at us as if we're strangers. "Why is she crying?"

"She's—well, she's a little upset." I clear my throat.

"What about?"*Obaasan*'s eyes are blank, her gaze void of recognition.

I bite my lip, then offer the truest answer I can think of. "She...uh, lost her mom."

*Obaasan* sits silently for a moment. "I lost my daughter here too. She used to come and visit, but I haven't seen her in a long, long time." Her eyes grow teary again. "I miss her."

At this, Midori starts crying even harder, wracked with sobs until she's nearly folded in two on the concrete garden bench. "I should have come more often. Maybe then she'd—"

"Don't cry, child." *Obaasan* reaches out a trembling hand and brushes Midori's knee. "My Midori was always strong, even through her tears. Be strong today."

Midori lifts her head, mascara pouring down her cheeks. She sniffles, then reaches out to take *Obaasan*'s hand before speaking in a rapid stream of Japanese. *Obaasan* replies, her words slower and more tenuous than Midori's.

Brander reaches out and tugs on my hand, drawing away me from the bench. He bows his head, as if to pray. So that's what we do—together.

"Do you think you'll visit her again?" The words tiptoe from my mouth as we drive home later that afternoon. "I think she'd like to see you more often."

"But would I like to see her?" Midori closes her eyes long enough to convince me that she's going to rear-end the surf beater in front of us. Thankfully she opens them in time to slam on the brakes at a red light. "Every time I visit it's as if I lose a little more hope."

"What about the wedding? I really want her there." Even if she snores the whole time, *Obaasan* needs to be included. She's as much *ohana* as anyone.

Midori rubs her temples with one hand as the light changes and she guns her motor. "The thought of having her at the wedding, there but also not, is...too much."

"But she can at least be there as much as she could be. Why can't you give her that chance? I'd kill to have my mom at the ceremony, no matter where her mind was."

Midori hums under her breath, as if considering that for a moment. "I can't make that commitment right now."

"Fine." I lean against my seat. "But keep an open mind."

*God, I want* Obaasan *at my wedding, no matter what it takes. She needs to be there. For me, for Brander...and for Mindoro. You can make that happen, right?*

It's a long shot, I know. But hey—talking to God never hurts.

# Chapter Sixteen

"DRESS?"

"Check."

"Bouquet?"

"Check."

I mark off the two corresponding boxes on the custom-designed spreadsheet and peek up at Midori. She didn't text me once all week after we visited *Obaasan*, and her normally shiny-eyed expression—the one that means business—is dull today. Even so, something in her expression seems softer, more open. Maybe the visit with *Obaasan* was a good thing after all.

"We're starting to make headway here, girls." She taps a fountain pen against her leather journal. "What should we do next?"

"What about take a *break*?" Macie groans from where she's stretched out on the Delacroixs' couch and rolls over onto her stomach, plopping her sandy feet on a designer throw pillow. Jazz gives her a poke, and Macie yelps before sitting up and dropping her feet to the floor. "Seriously though, we've been going over stuff for hours. I'm bored."

Midori bites her lip. "We still haven't chosen processional music—or the decor for the ceremony. And what about wedding favors? We're running out of time!"

"Midori." Gramma looks up from her armchair, where she's been leafing through a bridal magazine. "The wedding is months away. There's plenty of time."

"But..."

"Gramma's right." I reach across the coffee table and pluck the fountain pen from Midori's hand. "We could all use a break. Besides—as long as we have one thing figured out, I'm happy."

"What's that?"

"The groom."

As if on cue, Brander walks in, followed by Hunter, whose gaze is unusually sober. Not even the sight of Jazz brings a smile to his face. *Uh-oh.* "I figured I'd find you guys here." Brander offers a wave and drops a quick kiss on my head. "What's up?"

"Nothing. Absolutely nothing." Macie slides off the couch and crashes to the floor with a thud. "I thought we were going to do something cool today like talk about the catering. All your mom wants to do is go over her checklist. For the *millionth* time."

"Macie..." Gramma's tone carries more than a hint of warning.

Macie *harrumphs* under her breath. "Sorry." She pulls herself back onto the couch. "But I'm *bored.*"

Brander shuffles his bare feet against the plush white carpet and shoves his hands deep in his pockets. "I thought you'd be planning a bridal shower or bachelorette trip or something."

"Bachelorette trip? What about a bachelor trip, huh?" Hunter tugs on his sagging manbun, his voice lacking its usual jovial lilt. "I've always wanted to go deer hunting on Molokai."

"Deer hunting?" Brander visibly pales. "Dude, just because your name's Hunter that doesn't mean you need to live up to it."

"Aw, man." Hunter snaps his fingers and hangs his head, a ghost of a smile flitting across his face. "It was worth a try."

"Well, then." Midori clears her throat, her own face looking a bit pale. "You gentlemen can discuss this another time. In all actuality, though, a bachelorette trip should be in the works."

"A bachelorette trip, Midori?" Gramma's eyes grow wide. "Isn't that a little—"

"It's perfect!" Midori claps her hands and lets out a squeak, the first expression of pleasure I've seen from her since we visited *Obaasan* last week. "It's the ideal solution. You girls can go off on vacation while I finish making arrangements for the reception. When you return, you'll be refreshed and ready to finalize the important details."

Ten pounds of stress drop from my chest at the thought of letting Midori handle things on the home front for a while, but at the same time... "That doesn't seem very fair to you."

Midori shushes me with a flick of her wrist. "I've planned more events than most people attend in an entire lifetime. I'll take care of every practicality while you're out of town—and I know the perfect place for you to go."

"Really?" Jazz's eyes light. "Where?"

Midori stays silent a moment, a smile blooming on her face. I'm surprised she hasn't already dialed her travel agent. "Girls, have any of you ever been to Las Vegas?"

"I can't believe I let your mom talk us into going to Vegas. What even?" I lean into Brander as we stroll along the shore after church on Sunday. "I mean, Sin City? I have enough problems of my own right here in Lahaina, thank you very much."

Brander smothers something that sounds suspiciously like a laugh. "Vegas isn't so bad. We have a sister resort there, right on the strip."

"*Strip*?"

Brander chuckles again, as if he's in on some sort of private joke. "It's where all the big casinos are. Our sister resort is—"

"Resort? As in…"

"It's kind of a casino too." Brander shrugs. "But a nice one. There's plenty to do there other than drink, smoke, and gamble. You'll have a great time, guaranteed."

"I sure hope so." A wave sweeps forward and crashes over our toes, spraying onto my legs.

"I know so." Brander offers a smile, but it wobbles around the edges. "I'm sure going to miss you."

"Miss me? You'll be so busy planning that orthopedic convention and jamming with Hunter that you won't even notice I'm gone." *Unless you two decide to jet off to Nashville instead.* That, I suppose, would be an even bigger distraction.

Almost as if he can read my mind, Brander draws me over to a downed palm and pats the trunk for me to sit. "There's something I should tell you." His voice is softer, stripped of its previous teasing tone.

"What's wrong?"

"Nothing. But Hunter and I had a conference call with Mike yesterday. We were going to tell everyone the news, but then Mom got excited about Vegas and—"

"And what?"

Brander ducks his head low. Doesn't say a word.

My heart hiccups. Nerves pulse. *This is it.*

The trill of a bird sounds overhead. Ocean waves pound

in my ears. *Say something*. I don't know if that command is for me or Brander or both of us, but my tongue stays glued to the roof of my mouth like the wallpaper in Gramma's guest bathroom. Considering the torrent of thoughts and questions swirling around in my heart like a tropical cyclone, though, maybe that's for the best.

Finally, Brander opens his mouth to speak. "We said no."

"You—*what*?" Half of me is ready to do a happy dance and start unpacking my mental suitcase, but the other part—the saner side of my brain—is frozen.

Brander gave up his dream.

Again.

"But why?"

"We both prayed about it. Hunter didn't hear anything either way."

"And you did?"

"*You* did." Brander's cheeks flush. "I know how much you love it here. How you don't want to leave."

I gape at him, stomach spinning.

I should be happy. I *know* I should be happy.

Why am I not happy?

"Let me get this straight. You based your decision on a once-in-a-lifetime-opportunity on *my* vote?"

"Yes." Brander wraps his arms around me. "I want you to be happy—always. There's no way on earth I'd ever do anything to jeopardize that."

Brander's embrace, the hug that normally feels so comforting, is nearly enough to smother me. I pull away. "But Hunter..."

"He's fine." There's a smile on Brander's face, but I'm not sure I believe it—or him. "He wouldn't want to leave his family any more than I'd want to leave you. There'll be other opportunities. I'm sure of it." He stands and pulls me up after him. "Come on, let's get a shave ice."

And so we do. Our usual giant rainbow cone is as delicious as always, but all the saccharine-sweet syrup in the world couldn't take away the creeping feeling in my chest right now.

Something deep in my heart is stirring. Weeping. Crying out.

*Brander made the wrong choice.*

"Gramma!" I barrel through the front door as soon as Brander drops me off and run straight into the kitchen. It's hot inside, and the air is decidedly sugar scented. Which makes sense, considering the thick, creamy icing Grams and Macie are squirting onto two dozen cupcakes spread on the counter. "Brander is an idiot! No, wait—*I'm* an idiot."

"What?" Gramma lays aside her piping bag and stares at me.

Macie keeps her bag in hand and shoots me a loaded glance as she swirls frosting atop a cupcake with a quick flick of her wrist. "You're not supposed to be here. Go away."

"Gee, thanks Mace. Let's focus on the task at hand, shall we? I don't know if that stupid job of Brander's has addled his brain or what, but he's going to ruin his life if he doesn't watch out." I pace the hall between the kitchen and dining room, one step away from pulling my hair out. "He gave up the record deal, Grams—for me."

Gramma drops the cupcake she's holding and it falls, icing-side down, on the sparkling clean countertop. "He *did*?"

"You'd better believe it." My frustration nearly boils over

at the thought of Brander picking up the phone, dialing Mike's number, and telling him no thanks. If only I hadn't made such a scene that night Brander got the call, maybe then things would be different. He would be halfway to becoming a star. To doing what he was meant to do. "He said he loves me and wants to make me happy. I guess he figured giving up his dream was the best way to do it. *I* think it's the stupidest thing ever."

"How sweet." Macie's voice laced with sarcasm as she picks up another cupcake. "So you're happy now then, right?"

"No! I—I..." The words die on my tongue and I sink to the floor before burying my head in my knees.

"Olive, you're acting like a two-year-old. Gramma, get her out of here and talk some sense into her. I need to finish frosting these things before the icing melts. Why does Hawaii have to be so dang hot?" Macie's voice drifts down to meet me on the floor.

"Don't say *dang*," I correct her automatically, but I doubt the words have their usual impact considering I just paraded through the kitchen muttering about stupid idiots.

"Sorry." Macie sounds anything but, and silence descends over the kitchen for a moment before soft footsteps pad across the room and a warm hand rests on my head.

"Let's go out front."

I look up to find Gramma's kind, tender-eyed gaze fixed on me. She offers her hand, and I take it before standing and following her outside, feeling very much like the two-year-old I'm supposedly acting like.

"I feel terrible—absolutely horrible, Grams. Brander should've signed with Mike. I'm holding him back."

"Do you think he feels the same way?"

"How should I know? Isn't this the kind of stuff we're supposed to talk about in premarital counseling?" I twist my engagement ring around and around my finger. "All Jonah has us doing is taking quizzes on each other's love languages and that kind of junk."

"Hmm." Gramma smooths her muumuu, her crepey hands in stark contrast with its smooth, plumeria-print silk. "Maybe you should talk to him see if there isn't a different course you could work through."

"I guess it doesn't matter—not as much as this, anyway. I can't believe Brander said no. He'd have to be happier making music in Nashville than slaving away in the salt mines here."

"Salt mines?"

"His dad is running him ragged. It's not fair."

"Have you talked to Brander about *that*?"

"No." I hang my head.

"What about Jesus? How much of this does He know?"

I swallow hard. "Because He's all-powerful and all-knowing and omnipotent? All of it."

"And because you've talked to Him about it and sought His will..."

"None of it." I rest my head in my hands. "I'm sorry, Grams." *And I'm sorry, God.*

Gramma's hand rests upon my back, and she pats it gently, the same way Mom used to when I was upset. "Marriage isn't easy, Olive. It will stretch you and Brander more than you might imagine. There will be times when he irritates you—and I think we both know you'll irritate him."

"Thanks for the vote of confidence. What does that have to do with anything?"

"Just an observation. A marriage built on the illusion of

happily ever after is weak. Neither you nor Brander are perfect—a fact you'll be well aware of soon enough. With only a human-sized love holding it together, your marriage could crumble over a single disagreement."

I bite my lip. That truth hurts, but there's something I can do to change it. There must be. "Then what can hold us together?"

Gramma simply points up.

"You're talking about God's love, aren't you? And probably prayer too."

"Sounds like a wise answer to me." A smile that I would call smug coming from anyone other than Gramma tickles her lips.

"Me? Wise? I doubt that. But maybe talking to God about all of this *would* make things better."

We fall into silence, the swing swaying a bit in the languid afternoon, a breeze rushing through the plumeria bushes beneath the porch. An extra-strong gust of wind brings forth a burst of Mom's smell, that sweet plumeria-and-sea-breeze scent she somehow managed to find in a bottle, and her words seem to twine around my heart.

*True love is a sacrifice.*

"Hey, Grams?" I look over at her. "Did Mom write me any more letters? You know, like the one you gave me at the dress shop?"

Gramma bites her lip and twiddles her thumbs in her lap—in other words, yes. I wait for her confirmation, but it doesn't come.

"Are you not supposed to tell me or something? I'm sure Mom wouldn't mind, considering the circumstances."

Gramma's eyes dart from me to the sea and back again. "I don't know..."

"Think on it, okay?" I hop up from the swing and give Grams a pat. "But, until then, I have some work to do."

I head upstairs, bare feet thumping against the worn bamboo flooring, the smell of Macie's cupcakes still heavy in the air, and head to my room. I flop onto my bed and shut my eyes to pray, but any words I thought I had for God jam in my brain.

How can they not? All my mind's eye can see is a record contract with Brander and Hunter's names on it getting crumpled up and thrown in the trash.

Over and over and over again.

# Chapter Seventeen

"GALLOWAY." MARK LEANS INTO MY cubicle at five minutes till quitting time on Monday afternoon, a frown on his face. My neck tightens. Mark only calls people by their last name when he's mad.

*Mad at me?*

"The journalist for our fall feature story bailed on me."

"Oh. Wow." I tug at a loose thread on my shirt. "That's too bad."

"Not for you. Ready for your first front-cover byline?"

"For real?" My heart gives a skip. No more writing about endangered seals or zillion-year-old trees? No more finding ways to make paid advertisements look like feature articles? No more proofreading columns that are so bad I have to fight the urge to rewrite them myself? "What's the story?"

"A good one. If you put the right spin on it, you'll have readers in tears." Mark tosses a double-stuffed folder onto my desk.

"Tears, huh?" Mark isn't usually one to go for sob stories.

"Tears." Mark nods, his goatee brushing the collar of his oversized Hawaiian-print shirt. "I'm leaving tomorrow to do gather info for a review of that new all-inclusive resort in Wailea. Read over this, get an outline drawn up, and we'll talk when I get back."

Leave it to Mark to snag the best assignments for himself—but, at the same time, I'll take what I can get. And this story sounds like a good one. "Thanks, Mark."

"You're welcome. I'm not usually one to hand this kind of thing off to a newbie, but I've got a good feeling about you, Galloway. You'd better not let me down."

"I won't." I stare at the overflowing folder, then at the back of Mark's balding head as he stalks out of my cubicle.

*I'd better not.*

When I get home, Gramma's car isn't in the driveway, and the house is closed up tight.

No note.

No text.

Nothing.

I'm contemplating whether I should call the cops to report a kidnapping by the world's neatest burglar or Jazz to see if she wants to hang out when my phone makes the decision for me.

"Olive! It's an emergency." Jazz sounds awfully excited for there to be any real emergency, but I play along.

"What's wrong?"

"You'll see—just come!"

"Come where, exactly?"

"Just *come!*"

At that moment, the doorbell rings. "Wait a second, Jazz, someone's—"

"See ya soon!" The line goes dead, leaving me shaking my head as I open the door.

"Brander?" I find him on the front porch, dressed way nicer than I am and holding tight to an overstuffed gift bag. "What's going on? Does this have anything to do with Jazz?"

"You think I'm going to tell you?" He shakes his head

and holds up the bag. "Here. We need to hurry if we don't want to be late."

"Hurry *where*? I'm not even dressed right."

"How do you know that if you don't even know where you're going?"

"Because *you're* dressed so nice."

"That's why I'm supposed to give you this." Brander hands me the bag. "Go get changed, but *hurry*."

I tear into the bag the second I'm safely in my bedroom, pawing past a white sundress with a broad peach sash, matching shoes, and a tube of lip gloss for some sort of clue as to what on earth is happening. Brander didn't decide we should elope after all, did he?

And then, there it is.

At the bottom of the bag lays an envelope with my name on it. My name, written in someone's oh-too-familiar handwriting.

*Mom.*

I can barely open the envelope fast enough, but I'm careful not to rip the letter inside as I pull it out.

*Hello, sweet girl, and happy wedding-shower day!*

Wedding shower?

I set the note aside and start unbuttoning that dress.

"Finally!" Jazz hurls herself at me, her prosthesis glinting from beneath the short leg of her blue seersucker jumpsuit. "What did you do, take a tortoise?"

"No, but you grossly overestimate my hairdressing

abilities." I point to my hair, which I barely managed to coax into a semi-cute, very-messy bun before Brander drove me out to the Wahikuli Beach Park—the same place where he proposed. "What is all of this?"

"It's your wedding shower, of course!" Jazz spreads her arms wide and cheers.

The park is packed nearly as full as when people gather to watch the annual Lahaina Paddleboard Race, and a million paper lanterns hang from the trees overhead. Hunter is setting up some sort of African-style box drum next to where Brander's guitar already hangs from a stand. Gramma and Macie are presiding over a picnic table laden with food, including those cupcakes they'd been fussing over yesterday. But nothing catches my eye more than a picnic table at the other end of the park. It's piled with gifts—so many that my fingers start to ache at the mere thought of untying all those ribbons.

"Happy four-months-to-go, Olive." Brander bends to plant a kiss on my lips—one that makes my cheeks grow a little warm considering how many people there are around. Public displays of affection aren't usually my thing, but on a night like tonight...

I let my eyes follow Brander across the park as he runs to join Hunter at the makeshift bandstand. They start to play, first upbeat background music, then their breakout single—the same one that, I'm sure, made Mike want to sign them.

"Earth to Olive." Jazz tugs on the sash of my dress. "This is your wedding shower. You're supposed to be having fun."

"I am. But...did Hunter tell you?" I keep my voice low enough for Brander's vocals to cover the tightness in my tone.

"Hunter? Why do you always assume that Hunter and I—"

"I'm not assuming anything. He and Brander nixed the record deal."

"What? No!" Jazz's voice creeps up a bit too high, and a few ladies from church glance our way.

"Shh. We can talk later." I turn my chin toward the stage. "But I think Hunter's pretty bummed."

"Oh." Jazz's expression falls, like she's disappointed for him—a little more disappointed than she'd be for any other friend. "In that case, it's up to us to put him in a better mood. I know exactly what we need to do."

Before Jazz gets her chance, we have to make it through an evening of food, gifts, and a bunch of ridiculous games that have me and Brander going head-to-head to correctly answer the most trivia questions about each other. Who actually remembered that one of our first conversations had something to do with the words "crazy booger" anyway?

Finally, though, Jazz gets to put her plan into action.

Macie is still presiding over the dessert table like the queen of cupcakes, making sure everyone knows that the offerings were homemade in her own kitchen, but the rest of the wedding party somehow manages to sneak away from the action. We find a quiet place on the seawall and sit in the impending twilight.

Our legs—both real and man-made—dangle high above the surf, and Brander's hand finds my own as the sun inches toward the horizon.

"So, Brander." Jazz leans around me to talk to him, but her eyes wander over to Hunter, who's sitting silently on

Brander's other side. "When are you going to have the bon-fire? During the ceremony or at the reception?"

"What?" Brander shakes his head at her. "What are you talking about?"

"Come on, you remember." Jazz laughs. "The bonfire? With all the girls' numbers you used to get after singing at youth group?"

"Whoa, dude. What's this?" A glimmer of interest eclipses the melancholy look on Hunter's face, and he digs his elbow into Brander's side. Brander, on the other hand, looks less than amused.

I clear my throat to mask a snicker as the memory floats back to me on a wisp of salt-scented sea breeze. "Brander swore he had so many girls' numbers that he could start a bonfire with them when he finally got married."

"Not *could*." Jazz waves a finger in the air. "*Would*. He kept them in a special box and everything."

"Dude!" Hunter slaps his thigh. "That's epic. So when are you doing it?"

"In your dreams." Brander shakes his head. "I pitched the numbers when I moved into my apartment. They're covered under a million pounds of trash in the Olowalu dump by now."

"Actually, you're forgetting who helped you move. The box is in my closet." A smile stretches the corners of Jazz's mouth nearly to her ears. She looks more pleased than a cat who broke into a canary store for a major feeding frenzy. "I've been printing out some of the weirdest comments girls have left on your social media posts for Anchor too. Just to keep it fresh. There's *more* than enough for a bonfire by now."

"What?" This time, Brander's whole body goes tense.

"How?"

"You really thought I'd help you move just for the fun of it?" Jazz's smile only gets bigger.

"Dude." Hunter shakes his head and offers Jazz a high-five, which she readily returns.

"You should come over sometime and check it out, Hunter—we could look up some of the girls up. Find you a date for the wedding. But that's beside the point. Ceremony or reception, Brander?"

"Neither." Brander blushes so immediately and completely that anyone walking by would instantly peg him for a sunburnt tourist. "I'm over that."

"No way, man." Hunter is laughing so hard he can barely get the words out. "We are *totally* doing this."

"No we're not!" Brander might be chuckling, but there's panic in his eyes. "It was a dumb thing from high school. Help me out, Olive?"

"Nope. Your big bonfire was one of the first things you told me about when I met you—"

"Because Jazz *forced* it out of me." Brander does his best to look angry, but the upward tilt of his lips belies the irritated spark in his eye.

"Doesn't matter. A true man always keeps his word." I cross my arms and lift my chin like I won the round. "You want to make me happy? Start gathering timber."

One quick glance at Hunter reveals that Jazz's plan was a success. He's still half-doubled over in laughter, all of his melancholy seemingly forgotten.

For now.

But what happens tomorrow and the next day and the next, when Jazz isn't around to cheer him up?

Either Brander needs to reconsider that record deal, or

I need to get Hunter and Jazz on the fast-track to happily ever after.

Or, preferably, both.

# Chapter Eighteen

"I'm home!" I drop my work bag, overstuffed with a week's worth of journalistic junk, on the entryway floor with a bang. Zuzu, Macie's pup, leaps from her spot on the floor and starts howling like someone shot a gun at her.

It's been five long days of proofreading interns' articles and finalizing only the most boring wedding details, and it still isn't over. That file-folder of information on the fall feature article isn't going to read itself, and Brander and I have a premarital counseling date with Jonah at the Shave Ice Shack tonight.

"Why are you banging around like an angry water buffalo?" Macie pops out of the kitchen, a skiff of flower dusting her cheeks and chin. "You'd better stop or my cake's going to fall. It's a new recipe, and it's very important."

"More cake, Mace?" I groan. "At the rate you're going, I'm not going to be able to fit into my wedding dress."

"Not my problem. I need to keep testing recipes so I can—"

My phone cuts her off with an urgent buzz, and I glance at the screen. Mark. "Uh-oh."

"Are you in trouble?" Macie squints at me, but the oven timer screeches at her before I can respond. She takes off like a miniature rocket ship, leaving me with no other choice than to answer the phone.

*Please don't ask about the article, please don't ask about the article, please don't—*

"Galloway!" Mark's voice booms through the phone, but at least he doesn't sound mad. "How's that article coming?"

"It's...coming."

"Good, good, because I have a scoop for you. What are you doing right now?"

"Why do you ask?"

"Because you've got an exclusive interview with Mr. Murphy himself at six o'clock. This is big."

"Who's Mr. Murphy?"

"Hank Murphy? The owner? The one you're doing the story on? Come on, Galloway." There's that edge in his voice—the serrated one.

"*That* Hank. Sorry, Mark. It's been a long day." Why didn't I make myself skim through that folder sometime earlier in the week? I'm going to go down looking like the island idiot if I don't get my act together. "Where's this interview? And when?"

"Shave Ice Shack. As soon as you can get there. And pull yourself together, Galloway. This one's going to be big."

"Hey." Why is talking to Brander's answering machine always so much harder than talking to him in real life? "Change of plans. I have to do an interview with this guy at the Shave Ice Shack before we can meet with Jonah, okay?" I pause, as if waiting for some sort of answer, but of course that's ridiculous. "Okay. Bye."

Thank goodness I'm a magazine journalist and not a radio host.

I pull into the Shave Ice Shack parking lot and snag my favorite spot—the one where Brander used to park his moped when we worked here together. I have five minutes before my scheduled interview time, so I grab the folder Mark gave me and give it a quick skim.

The guy I'm going to be interviewing is indeed the owner of the Shave Ice Shack, Hank Murphy. The same guy who put me on probation on my second day of work. I flip forward a few pages. Hopefully he's long since forgotten about that incident, because I'm going to be interviewing him about—

*No.*

I blink at the page, my vision suddenly quavering. This can't be right.

There's no way on Maui or Mars that I'm going to march on up to the counter, ask to speak to Hank and interview him about...the Shave Ice Shack closing.

"Sorry, kid, but it's the truth." Hank—the same guy who was my grumpy boss for years and scared me out of my wits every time he showed up when I was on the clock—stares at me with hollowed-out eyes, his dark skin accented by the shadow cast by an overhead palm tree. He looks older than I remembered, and the tattoos that used to stretch across his biceps now hang limp. Basically, he seems to have aged fifty years in the last five. "My lease is up in September, and there's no way I can sign it again. Not with my wife's condition the way it is."

"Let me get this straight." I stare at the pages of notes that I've scribbled, then at my on-the-house shave ice, now half-melted. A flicker of guilt whispers that I should at least take a bite, but my stomach hasn't stopped swimming since I got here. "Your wife's had ALS for the last—"

"Three years." Hank clasps his hands together, fingers interlocked, and raises them to his lips. "I was ready to throw in the towel the day we got the diagnosis, but she refused. Said the one thing I could do to make her life better was to keep the place afloat. She loves hearing all the stories about the regulars. But now..." His voice cracks. "The doctors say we don't have much time left. I don't want to waste another minute that I could spend with her. We're shutting down at the end of the summer."

My own throat grows thick. I stare at my own hands, sitting solidly on the weathered picnic table. I should be taking more notes, but how can I give this story the coverage it deserves when my own heart is breaking?

It's bad enough that we're losing the best shave ice shack on the island. Does Hank have to lose his wife too?

I glance at my folder, at the list of questions that the other reporter had compiled. "Have you thought about selling the shack?" My voice is wobbly, but I have to push through. Have to get the answers I need to make this story a success—for Hank and his wife, if nothing else.

Hank shakes his head. "We had a good run, me and this old place, but our time is up. At the end of the day, this business isn't about the money. It's about the people—the customers we served and the kids we helped out. There's more to shave ice than a secret recipe. It's the aloha spirit that makes it sweet. Some big chain could buy me out, but this place would never be the same."

It's those words that follow me throughout the rest of the interview, twining around my heart like a snake and pulling so tight that I feel like I'm about to break.

*This place will never be the same.*

"Hey, Olive." Jonah greets me with a shaka-fisted wave when he shows up at the shack minutes after Hank and I finish our interview. "Everything okay?"

I shake my head first, then nod. Hank made it clear that this story is an exclusive—for the *West Maui Sun* only—and it can't break until the September issue hits newsstands. That doesn't mean I'm not planning on telling Brander, Jazz, and maybe even Gramma before then, but Jonah? He'll have to wait and read it for himself.

"I'm fine."

"You're sure about that?" Jonah waggles one bushy eyebrow. "Nothing you need to get off your chest?"

"Actually…" I bite my lip. I can't in good conscience tell him about my talk with the manager of the Shave Ice Shack, but I *can* get an opinion on something else.

I make quick work of telling him about Brander and Hunter's decision on the record deal, my pulse thundering in counterpoint with my words. How could I have ever tried to get between them and their dream?

"I'm an idiot." I rest my arms on the table and bury my head in my hands. Sure, maybe I'm being overdramatic, but this is Brander's future we're talking about. If Hank is willing to give up the Shave Ice Shack to spend the last few months of his wife's life with her, then I should be willing to move to Nashville with Brander.

"After all, isn't that what true love is? Giving up everything you have to make the other person happy?" I barely realize I've spoken the words aloud until Jonah offers a reply.

"Yes and no." He locks his fingers together and stretches, placing his hands behind his head and leaning against the bench. "We've all been called to the kind of self-sacrificing love that Jesus has for His followers, but that kind of love is deep. We're not meant to be each other's comfort, joy, or happiness."

"Wait a minute." Maybe I should be taking notes here

too. "Then what *are* we supposed to be?"

"Guides. Friends. Traveling companions along the road of life—we're called to be all this and more. But we cannot, under any circumstances, be burdened by another person's emotions. That's God's territory. *He* is the only one who can bring true happiness."

"But...isn't true love and joy and happiness what the honeymoon phase is all about?"

Jonah chuckles. "You're getting way ahead of me, here. That's supposed to be our last talk together—the one right before your wedding. And ideally the groom is present for this as well."

"But—"

"Don't worry. I'll give you the short version. The honeymoon phase is a lie—part wishful thinking, part human emotion. Even at your finest, you and Brander can't make each other happy all of the time. It doesn't work like that. Sure, at the beginning of your marriage you'll find each other's unique quirks and habits less annoying than you might later on, but that true, unadulterated joy you'll find as a couple comes only from the Lord."

"But—"

"God has commanded us to honor and serve one another, but we can't be responsible for each other's happiness all day, every day. It's not what we're called to."

Jonah reaches for his Bible and flips through the pages, as if looking for a verse to help me make sense of all this, but he's interrupted by the urgent beeping of my phone. I answer the call and put it on speaker.

"Olive!" Brander is practically yelling. "I—I'm being kidnapped."

"Wait, what?" I stare at the phone on the picnic table.

"You'd better say that again, because it sounded like you said you were being kidnapped. And I'm not rich enough to pay any sort of ransom money."

Brander laughs, and the sound of his voice spills out of the phone like a ribbon of sweetened condensed milk pouring from a can. "Don't worry, there's no ransom. But I'm not going to be able to make it to counseling."

"Why not?"

"I told you—I'm being kidnapped!" Brander laughs again. There sure is a lot of kidnapping going around lately, what with all this getting-married business. "My dad's buddy is the manager at the Four Seasons resort on Lanai. They're having a big music festival this weekend, and one of the headlining acts cancelled."

"Let me guess—this manager guy called in a favor?"

"It gets better. Dad sprung for a room there for a whole week. No conference-scheduling, no phone calls, no work. I guess Hunter and I are getting our bachelor trip after all." He sounds so excited I'm surprised he isn't calling to say his and Hunter's latest single hit the top of the music charts.

"That sounds great." I put on a smile, and it seems to come out in my words, but even so...

Something shuffles on Brander's end of the line. "I'm sorry to leave you and Jonah hanging. I would've told you earlier if I knew. I could see if I could catch a late ferry so we can—"

"Are you kidding? And spoil your bachelor trip? Have a great time. I—I'll talk to you when you get home." There's no way I can drop the bomb about the Shave Ice Shack now. Not in front of Jonah, and especially not with Brander about to leave on the trip of a lifetime.

I guess a late-night powwow with Grams is in order.

# Chapter Nineteen

I PHONE HOME AND PUT IT on speaker the second I get in the car that evening. I'm halfway out of the packed parking lot—Friday night is prime shave ice time, apparently—when Gramma answers.

"Hello?" A bunch of plates and glasses clink in the background.

"Grams, we have a problem."

"We do?" Something rustles, almost like she's stretching the cord of her clunky landline in the hall around the corner and into her bedroom. The sound of chatter and clanking dishes fades. "A big problem, or an I'm-going-to-blow-this-out-of-proportion kind of problem?"

"An actual problem. Brander got kidnapped to go do this concert on Lanai, but I really need to talk to him because I have this assignment at work, and the Shave Ice Shack manager's wife has ALS and—"

"Gramma!" Macie hollers so loud on the other end that it's like she's in the car next to me, bellowing in my ear. "Zuzu threw up on Kanani's sleeping bag!"

"Wait, do we have company?"

Gramma sighs, sounding much older and more world-weary than a grandmother should sound—even one that's put up with me for the last six years. "Macie's having a slumber party. I'd better go help them. I'm sure everything'll be fine, sweetie. You wait and see."

"But you don't understand! The Shave Ice Shack is—"

"*Gramma!*" Macie's voice is even louder this time, and I barely catch Gramma's hasty goodbye before the call disconnects with a click. So much for spilling my heart out.

And, considering that the house is now overrun with a bunch of preteen girls, I'm not sure I want to go home. I flip a U-turn and, before I know it, I'm pulling in front of the doggie-rescue mission.

*Jazz, you're my only hope.*

"Jazz?" Dani's eyes widen when I ask her about the whereabouts of my friend. "She's out on an—um, she's on an errand."

"An errand?" I peer past Dani into the house's living area, but she blocks my view with her football-linebacker shoulders. The Polynesian woman isn't much taller than me, but boy, is she buff. I guess you'd have to be, wrestling with pit bulls all day long and surfing on your off hours. "That's okay. I don't mind waiting."

Dani bites her lip. "She won't be back until late."

"How late?"

"Too late to hang out with you." Dani folds her arms and huffs. "Funny, she told me you were going to be busy all night."

"Why would she tell you that?"

"Never mind." Dani waves a hand in the air dismissively. "Come over tomorrow. You can talk then."

"Fine." My eyes are one twitch of a nerve away from rolling around and around in my head. "Thanks, Dani."

"Any time." She waves her fist in a *shaka* after me as I retreat to my car, and I return the gesture before climbing in and heading toward the only place I have left.

Brander's and my condo unit is still pretty empty, except for a few boxes of stuff that Brander and I got at our wedding shower, but that doesn't matter. I'm not going to be inside for long, anyway. I pull out my phone and order a personal-sized Pirate Pete's pizza before heading out on the lanai, where a teak bistro table—Midori and Auggie's gift to us—sits waiting.

The sun hovers over the horizon, a good half hour from setting. *Perfect.* A romantic sunset dinner...for one.

*Or maybe two.*

Brander might be halfway across the channel by now, but a girl's never too old for a dinner date with her dad.

Once my pizza arrives and I get settled out on the lanai, I prop up my phone and give Dad a buzz. He answers on the first ring. "Olive!" His voice is way too chipper for almost-midnight Boston time. "How are you? How goes the wedding planning? And what's this about a record deal?"

"Whoa, Dad. Take a breath. You didn't happen to drink any coffee today, did you?" I bite my lip, picturing Dad sitting alone in his apartment all day, grading papers and guzzling gallons of that nasty black sludge he and Gramma seem to adore. I've got to remember to call him more often.

"Coffee?" He lays a finger alongside his freshly-shaved chin—a far cry from the scruffy bird's nest he's been sporting off and on since Mom died. "Let me see..."

"Never mind. Which question do you want me to answer first?"

"Doesn't matter." He readjusts his glasses. "Tell me all."

I do as he asks and catch him up on everything—wedding planning, my visit with *Obaasan*, and how Brander rejected the record deal—in between bites of hot, steamy pizza, dripping in mozzarella, ham, and pineapple. The same combo that Macie used to call "bad news pizza" seems appropriate tonight, what with the impending closure of the Shave Ice Shack hanging over my head like a thundercloud over the West Maui Mountains.

Despite the last of "bad news pizza" lingering on my tongue, I do my best to end the call on a positive note. "At least I have my bachelorette trip to look forward to."

"Is that so?" Dad smothers a yawn. It's well past midnight his time, but he's still dressed for work in a crisp white shirt and spiffy tie. Maybe he had a late class tonight. "Where are you headed to?"

"Vegas, of all places." I smother a snort. Brander—and even Macie and Jazz—might be convinced that there's more to Sin City than meets the eye, but I'll believe it when I see it. "Brander's mom got us a suite at one of the big resorts. We're flying out on Friday."

"Next Friday? You don't say." Dad's eyes glaze over, and a hint of a smile slips onto his face. "What a remarkable coincidence."

"What? Don't tell me you're going to Vegas too."

"Actually, yes." Dad pushes up his glasses again. "Think you can take time out of your girls' weekend to spend some time with your dear old dad?"

"Of course! We should all meet for lunch. Macie'll be thrilled."

"Excellent." Dad's eyes twinkle. "There's a little place on the ground floor of the Venetian that your mom used to love."

"*Mom* went to Vegas?"

"She traveled there with me for an education convention

years ago. Didn't much care for it at first, but the place grew on her. Should I get us a table for five?"

"Four. Midori booked the trip, but she isn't coming with us."

"Yes, but there's someone who, ah..." Dad's face goes almost as red as the setting sun beyond my lanai. "There's someone I'd like you to meet. My friend."

"A friend, huh?" Speaking of red, flags of the same hue are going up in all corners of my brain. "Does this *friend* have a name?"

"Emily."

The word hangs there between us for a moment, so real I can practically see it swaying in the breeze, making me almost gag on my last bite of pizza—the same pizza that, like it or not, seems doomed to always forecast bad news.

"Is Emily a—"

"A visiting professor. From Oxford."

*Okay, then.* A visitor. Hopefully one who plans on heading back across the pond soon.

"She's going to be keynoting at the conference. Her plan is to move to the U.S. after completing her contract requirement, and this speaking engagement is the perfect chance for her to see more of the country." Dad clears his throat and loosens his tie. A tie that, come to think of it, is a little fancy even for a psychology lecture. Could it be that...

"Dad, do you have a *girlfriend*?" I gape at the screen. *No. Way.* Dad couldn't romance a wet paper bag if he tried. It's a miracle that Mom ever—

"Mom. What about Mom?"

"Don't jump to conclusions, Olive. Emily is a lovely woman, and I'm sure you'll enjoy getting to know her. She's a literature professor, you know. She grew up in Bath—Jane

Austen town, am I right?"

"You're...dating? Like, what Brander and I do? Like with flowers and chocolates and all that stuff?"

"Emily doesn't like chocolate, and I'm afraid flowers haven't crossed my mind. Now that you mention it—no, never mind. She's a friend. A very good friend, but a friend nonetheless."

"And you're going to *Vegas* together?" This time it's my words that hang in the air, almost like an accusation. I cringe at the idea of Dad and this Emily person making a quick detour through one of those drive-through wedding chapels. "I'm sorry, Dad. I'm sure she's a nice lady. This is just so...wow. This is a lot to take in."

"I should have figured as much." Dad clears his throat. "If it makes you feel any better, we're not exactly traveling together. In fact, we're staying on opposite ends of the strip."

I almost laugh at the absurdity of it all. It's like suddenly there's been a role reversal and *I'm* the parent. All the times Dad used to grill me about Brander flash through my mind, and suddenly I *do* laugh.

But tears are close to follow those few giggles—tears that I'm quick to hide from Dad.

Even so, I sit out on that lanai long after Dad and I say goodnight, staring at the darkening sky and the few stars that shine through the dusk like leftover pinpricks of sunlight.

*God, I need Your help.*

# Chapter Twenty

"DON'T LOOK, MACIE!" I SLAP MY hands over my little sister's eyes as a scantily clad showgirl struts down the Vegas strip in front of us. "I knew they called this place Sin City for a reason," I mutter to Jazz as Macie fights against my hands and nearly trips over a crack in the sidewalk.

"Olive, I can't *see!*" She wrenches away and instantly fixates on the lady. "What are you all worried about, anyway? I have swimsuits smaller than that dress."

"Yeah, Olive." Jazz giggles. "What's the big deal? *You* don't have to wear it."

"Good thing." I cross my arms and huff. I'd like to believe that it's the general demoralizing debauchery of the Las Vegas strip that's put me on edge, but it's probably more likely that our impending date with Dad and his—*Emily* that has me tied up in knots.

Or the fact that the Shave Ice Shack is closing and I'm still the only one who knows it. I must have tried to break the news a million times in the past week, but I can't bear to make myself voice the very words that will mark the end of one of Lahaina's sweetest eras. Not yet.

Better to pretend that the Shave Ice Shack will always be there, that Dad isn't dating, that...

"Olive? Where'd you go?" Jazz waves a hand in front of my face, and I swat it away. "Seriously, Midori wouldn't have sent us here if she thought it would be a bad experience. At least try to have fun, okay?"

"Fine. You're both right." And they are. The general atmosphere here in Sin City isn't any more outrageous than that on any given Hawaiian beach, and Vegas *is* admittedly beautiful. Maybe, if I could forget about everything for a few hours...

"Are you okay?" Jazz whispers in my ear, the words barely carrying over the chatter of what must be a thousand other tourists. "Your shoulders are still at cruising altitude."

"They are?" My shoulders plummet toward earth almost automatically. Our flight got in hours ago, but suddenly I feel as if I've actually landed. "Oh."

"Told you." Jazz snickers. "What's wrong?"

I gulp. Bite my lip. Jazz and Macie both know we're meeting Dad for dinner, but I conveniently forgot to mention anything about his "friend". Is it too late to tell them now?

We make our way along one side of the strip, popping into casinos designed to look like New York City, Paris, and even ancient Egypt. But between the clangs, clinks, and dings of the slot machines, the blaring music overhead, and the ticking time bomb in my brain, I can't say I'm having much fun.

"Okay, time out." Jazz turns and heaps half a pound of French fries on my otherwise-empty plate as we make our way down the line at what Midori assured us was the most opulent buffet in the entire city. "We're in Vegas, Olive. I don't know what's wrong with you, but it's not going to kill you to relax and have a good time. This place isn't evil—it's *fun.*"

"I know." I stare at a chocolate fountain—and the cookies, marshmallows, and other goodies ready to be dunked beneath the ribbon of hot fudge—as we head to our table. As good as all this food looks, the churning in my gut assures me that an attempt to eat any of it would end in disaster one way or another. "But...I need to tell you something."

Jazz bites her lip as she sits, and Macie follows her lead, though my little sister replaces the lip-biting with her own signature eye-rolling routine. "Olive, chill out. You're *always* stressing. It's getting annoying."

"So is your attitude. Since when does Gramma let you talk like that?"

"Is Gramma here?" Macie makes a big show of looking around the crowded restaurant. "Funny, I don't see her."

"Girls!" Jazz barks the word, her voice a frighteningly accurate replica of Gramma's. "If you want to fight, do it later. In front of an audience. I bet people here would pay big bucks to watch a wrestling match. Right now, I want to know what's bugging Olive."

"Dad has a girlfriend."

"*What?*" Jazz and Macie speak in unison so I can't tell which of them is louder. They must both be pretty loud, because half the other people in the dining room turn to look our way.

"Dad? A girlfriend?" Macie stares at her plate for a minute and fiddles with a fry, then looks up. "That's great!"

I almost choke on my own breath. "That's—"

"Yeah." Jazz unwraps her silverware from its napkin. "God didn't make us to live life alone."

"Well, I'm glad you're both happy, because you're going to be meeting her. Tonight." A sudden lump rises in my throat, and I pat my pocket, where the tiny envelop Gramma handed me before my flight—one with Mom's handwriting on it—still sits. Unopened.

*Poor Mom.*

"That's cool." Macie looks at her plate again. "Are we going to pray here or what? My food's getting cold."

"Hold on a minute, Macie." Jazz gives my sister's silky-smooth ponytail a tug. "This is important. Your dad said that—a girlfriend?"

"I think it was something more like 'my good friend Emily' but yeah. Basically, a girlfriend."

"You know that doesn't mean he loves your mom any less, right?"

This time I'm the one to roll my eyes. "Don't feed me that line, Jazz. It's a stupid platitude."

"What does a platypus have to do with anything?" Macie cocks her head at me like I've lost my marbles. It wouldn't be the first time. "Jazz is right. Dad still loves Mom—same as we do. Does that mean he should spend the rest of his life mooning over her when she's dead?"

"It just sounds so—so..."

"Don't get ahead of yourself." This time Jazz gives my own—equally shiny and smooth thanks to the merciful lack of humidity—ponytail a tug. "Give Emily a chance at dinner tonight, and we'll go from there. Now, let's pray."

Jazz doesn't give me time to object before she grabs my hand and Macie's and bows her head. "Dear God, I know change is hard. Please give Olive peace tonight, and help dinner to go well—"

"And," Macie cuts in, "help the rest of this trip to be *fun!* Amen. Let's eat."

Thankfully, the knot in my stomach loosens enough for me to fit in several trips' worth of buffet food—including approximately a gallon of fudge from that fountain—but it's still there, growing tighter and tighter as I count the hours until we'll meet Dad—and this Emily woman—for dinner.

"Girls!" Dad sweeps me into a hug that practically knocks me off my feet the second I step into the Venetian Hotel, filling me with a sudden rush of warmth that puts the triple-digits Las Vegas heat to shame. Macie is quick to throw herself into the mix. "How was your flight?"

"It was good." The warm fuzzies in my chest from Dad's hug turn to angry little fire ants when I pull away and see *her* standing behind him.

Emily.

She gives a little wave before crossing over to us. Her large, doe-like brown eyes rest squarely on me. Or, more accurately, the delicate collection of diamonds on my left ring finger.

"Congratulations on your engagement, Olive, and thanks for letting me and Alex crash your hen do. I've been hearing a lot about your young man. He sounds simply splendid." Her accent gives the words a certain lyrical quality, like she would make a good poet.

"Thanks." My mouth is suddenly dry, my breaths coming quicker. If this was any other woman, I'd be instantly intrigued. But she's...*Emily.*

As if picking up on what I'm thinking, Jazz bends and whispers in my ear the second Emily turns her attention to Macie. "You're allowed to like her, you know. Especially if she makes your dad happy."

I blink at Jazz. The words sound a little phony, like I've read them in one too many of those getting-over-grief shrinky-dink articles that Dad used to send me. But maybe...

I catch a flash of enamel on Emily's jacket lapel and squint at the small, rectangular pin. "Pemberley."

"Excuse me?" Emily turns toward me. She's a wisp of a thing—barely taller than I am, and that's saying something.

"Your pin. It's Pemberley, isn't it?"

"Ah, yes." Emily's cheeks flush pink, like guava syrup atop a cone of creamy white coconut shave ice. "Alex mentioned you were a fellow Janeite."

"A fellow *what?*" Jazz blinks at Emily, and Macie wrinkles her nose in my direction. "Sorry, but do you Harvard people speak a different language or something?"

"Not Harvard people—Jane Austen fans. Janeites are people who are obsessed with all things Jane Austen. Like us." I motion from myself to Emily, and we share a smile. A moment of solidarity. *Weird.*

"And Pemberley is a key setting in Jane's own *Pride and Prejudice.*"

"Not that book again." Jazz lays a hand to her heart, as if aghast at the thought of being reminded of her high school years. Before I know it, she's grabbed Macie's arm and dragged her over to the front of the restaurant. "Come on, let's see if they have a menu posted—at least that's a language *we* can understand."

"Thank you for being so gracious as to let me intrude upon your reunion with your dad—on your hen do, nonetheless." Emily tucks a strand of short, dark hair behind one shell-shaped ear and squares her feet.

I know I should either be reassuring her that her presence is a welcome one or telling her to steer clear of my dad and out of my already-anxiety-inducing life, but suddenly the only words on my tongue are... "What's a hen do?"

"Ah, right." Emily chuckles. "That's we call your

bachelorette trip across the pond." She clears her throat. "I hope I didn't impose."

"Not at all." I smile at her, and it feels strangely genuine. "It's nice to meet you."

"It is? Hmm." For a moment it's as if Emily is peering straight into my soul. "My father passed away when I was in lower sixth form. I didn't take too kindly to the thought of my mother dating again. I highly doubt you were too keen on meeting me."

"You've got that right." The admission rolls off my tongue before I can stop it. "*But*, since Dad's never actually said he's dating anyone, I'm perfectly happy to have dinner with his lady friend. She seems a lot nicer than most of the stodgy professors he usually hangs out with."

At this, a full grin breaks onto Emily's face, and her eyes sparkle. "Alex, I thought you said she'd be a hard sell." She swats Dad's elbow, and something in me cringes at the sight of them touching. But then Emily's Pemberley pin flashes again, and suddenly it's like Mom is standing right next to me, whispering in my ear.

*She's wonderful.*

And she kind of is.

The restaurant Dad picked must be a popular one, because it takes us half the evening to get in and another hour to get our food—but it's totally worth it.

Half-pound hamburgers are quickly devoured, all while Emily and Dad grill us about the wedding preparations. Jazz and Macie keep the conversation hopping—they've been more involved in the details anyway—giving me time to focus on my mozzarella, arugula, and tomato-trimmed burger.

Brander would totally love this place.

"So, Olive." Emily's pert, plucky voice breaks through my mini food coma, and I look up at her. Her arm brushes lightly against Dad's, but I'll give her the benefit of the doubt and assume that the booth is a little snug—though Jazz, Macie, and I have had no problem fitting into the other side. "What are you serving for your wedding breakfast? Did you pick an island theme?"

"Breakfast? Brander and I aren't getting married until sunset."

"Oops." Emily giggles into her hand. "We always refer to the reception meal as a wedding breakfast, no matter the time. Across the pond, it used to be the customary for the bride and groom to fast until after the wedding."

"*Oh*. In that case, I still don't know. Midori—Brander's mom—is planning the reception."

Emily's brows jump at that. "Why aren't you?" Her eyes glaze over slightly. "I've always wanted to plan a wedding."

"You mean you've never been married bef—ouch!" Macie yelps and cuts Jazz the stink eye. I'd bet good money that my little sister just received one of Jazz's signature pokes in the ribs. "*Sorry*. I'm just curious."

"Oh, I don't mind." Emily lays down her hamburger. "When I was in college, I was busy working several jobs, trying to help Mum stay on her feet after my father passed. After that...well, I suppose the right person never came along." Her cheeks are flushed pink now, and she stares at her burger and fries—er, chips, as I guess she'd call them.

A beat of awkward silence hangs between us, so palpable I'd like to pluck it right out of the air and pitch it in the nearest garbage can, until Emily leans across the table and hands me something. A...dime? "Um, thanks." Guess I could play one of those one-cent slot machines I keep seeing. "I guess."

"Alex, don't tell me you Yanks don't keep the old tradition?" Emily looks aghast, her mouth hanging in a perfect circle, but her tone is teasing.

"You mean the something old, something new thing?" Macie takes a massive bite of her burger and chews before finishing. "I get it—the dime is something borrowed. But what is Olive supposed to do with it?"

"No, not something borrowed. It's actually a sixpence, passed down in my family for generations. It's customary to put it in the bride's left shoe for good luck."

"Don't you want to keep it for yourself? For when—ouch!"

This time it's *Jazz* who is silenced with an elbow-poke of my own. "Thank you, Emily. I'll take good care of it for you. Until you need it." I wink across the table, and Emily's cheeks turn even pinker, like the outer petals of an English rose. Sitting next to Dad's long, lanky frame, she seems to fit. There's a part of my heart that kicks and screams against that observation, begging me to believe that no one less than Mom could ever take that place by Dad's side. But another part clings to what I know about Mom—about what she'd want.

And yet another part can't help wondering...if Mom wrote all of these letters for me, then maybe she wrote some for everyone else. Maybe even one for Dad.

"Gramma?" I keep my voice low as I talk into the phone. I snuck out of the restaurant with an excuse about stretching my legs before dessert, which Dad assures me will be the highlight of my trip, but all I care about is talking to Grams. So here I am, shoved in a corner between a vacant slot machine and the bathrooms, feeling strangely like a secret agent on a mission.

"Olive!" Gramma's voice crackles like the embers of a beachside bonfire, giving me a sudden wave of homesickness amidst the Vegas-style glitz and glam of the Venetian resort. "It's good to hear your voice, sweetie. The house seems so quiet with you girls gone. Though Brander and Midori have been making sure I'm not too lonely. Are you having fun?"

"A blast. Even though Dad brought a *lady friend* to dinner."

"He *what?*" Gramma's voice swoops up like a seabird taking flight, and I'm quick to explain.

"I didn't want to mention it—I was afraid it would spoil the trip. But it hasn't at all. Grams, Mom and Emily would've been best friends."

"Really?" Gramma's voice sounds skeptical, and I don't blame her. Maybe I shouldn't have announced it over the phone like this. It's not every day you learn that your daughter's husband is looking for a replacement. But Dad isn't getting married—*yet.*

"I called because I was wondering...Dad and Emily seem a little shy about the whole romance thing. I thought maybe Mom had written some letters for Dad. You know, so he wouldn't feel bad about dating again. Or maybe even one for Macie, to help her figure things out." Though, considering how easygoing Macie has been about this whole thing, I have a feeling that letter would be better suited for *me.*

Gramma stays quiet so long that I've nearly given up hope of any such letters existing when she finally clears her throat. "Yes, I believe there are. One for you—and Alex, Macie, and this new...Emily."

"That's great. We can hand them out at the wedding."

"Emily is coming to the wedding?" Gramma's voice shakes a bit.

"I'm assuming she is anyway. She gave me her six-pence."

"Her...what, now?" Gramma's voice sounds faint, as if all this news is suddenly too hard to take. Good grief, I hope all this stress won't give her a heart attack or anything. Maybe I should have Brander go over and check on her.

"I'm sorry, Grams. This was a bad time, wasn't it?"

"No, no sweetie. I'm a tough old bird—I can still take a few surprises now and then. Go enjoy your trip. We can talk later."

But as I finish the call and slip back into the restaurant where Dad, Emily, and the others are waiting—each holding a towering milkshake with an entire slice of pink-sprinkled confetti cake balanced precariously across the rim of the glass—I can't ignore the sudden pang in my heart, accompanied by the knowledge that it's time for me to stop relying on everyone else to fix my problems for me and *do something.*

Gramma has been carrying my burdens for way too long now—it's finally time for me to shoulder one of hers.

# Chapter Twenty-One

"RISE AND SHINE, LAS VEGAS, IT'S time for me to make my fortune!" Jazz swings her purse and breathes in deep, as if taking a moment to revel in the crisp desert-morning air as we step out on the strip bright and early the next morning.

"What do you mean? You're not seriously going to waste your money gambling, are you?" Midori gave each of us a sizable chunk of spending money before we left, but there's no way I'm feeding a single cent to one of those slot machines.

"Waste my money?" Jazz shakes her head. "Not a chance. But I don't consider taking ten bucks to spend on penny games a waste. You can't go to Las Vegas and not try your luck."

"But Jazz, luck is—"

"You don't have to play. Just keep me company, okay?"

"Then find a slot machine and get on with it." Macie gives Jazz a shove. "*I* want to go to the Fashion Show Mall."

We follow Jazz, who seems to be on a mission, all the way down the strip until we reach the Cosmopolitan—one of the ritziest resorts on the strip. "For real, Jazz?" I keep my voice well below a whisper as we step into a lobby area with a three-story-tall chandelier. "This place is ridiculous. Why can't we go somewhere else?"

"If I'm going to waste my money, at least I'm going to do it in style." Jazz tosses her pin-straight blonde hair, freed from its usual braid. It falls down her back like a rippling curtain of silk as she marches over to a slot machine.

Macie starts to follow, but I stop her with a tug on her elbow. "You're twelve, Mace. Not twenty-one. We'll stay right here."

"Wish me luck!" Jazz waves over at us as she sticks in her cash, and Macie raises both hands, fingers crossed. I do the same. Let Jazz have her fun. Pretty soon *I'll* be shopping.

Before Jazz can start the machine spinning, my phone pings in my pocket with a text. *Brander.* I snap a quick picture with Macie, then send it to him with a good-morning message. But I haven't even put my phone away before a squeal splits my eardrums.

"Olive!" Jazz hops on her good leg, waving both hands in the air. "You won't believe this!"

"Did you hit a jackpot?" Macie runs over before I can stop her, and I'm quick to follow. "Are you rich?"

"A-almost." Jazz points with one hand to the screen on the machine, where a digit followed by a healthy amount of zeros is flashing. "My first try too!"

A handful of gamblers swarm Jazz, offering her hearty high-fives and slaps on the back.

"Beginner's luck." A scrawny, wizened man shakes his head. "I'd stop now if I were you. Before the thrill of the pull takes over."

Jazz's eyes are bright, as if she's intoxicated by her sudden windfall, but she nods slowly, then a little faster before grabbing her ticket and heading for the cashier. She hurriedly accepts her money before linking her arms through mine and Macie's. "Come on, girls. Let's go shopping."

The three of us shop until we drop—quite literally—onto luxury loungers at some swanky-pants spa Midori recommended. By the time we've been massaged, seaweed-wrapped, and polished from head to toe, I feel like I, too, am capable of strolling the catwalk at the Fashion Show Mall.

"It's *so* not fair that they wouldn't give me a massage." Macie hunches over and picks at her sparkly pink manicure as we step back onto the strip. "I hate rules. And I hate not being sixteen."

"At least you got your nails done." Jazz stares at the ground as we walk, one hand clenched tightly around her purse strap.

"Is everything okay?" I nudge her with my elbow. "Or is that jackpot money starting to burn a hole in your pocket? Macie and I would be happy to take some of it off your hands if it's bothering you."

Jazz pinches her lips together. "Do you ever make bargains with yourself? Like, if X happens they I'll do Y and Z?"

"Um, no." Macie scrunches her nose. "Is that another one of those weird grown-up things?"

"Must be a weird *Jazz* thing." I wink at my friend. "What's up?"

"I told myself...okay, fine, I told myself *and* God that if I won a jackpot in Vegas, I'd do it." She lifts her chin, as if setting it, her resolve suddenly steely. "It's already all planned out."

Macie's brows jump nearly an inch up her forehead. "You mean you're finally going to ask Hunter—"

"*Macie,* shh!" I give her long, straight ponytail a tug. "Let her finish."

"We're going to take a little detour, and you guys have to hold my hand, okay?" Jazz fixes her gaze straight ahead, tromping down the strip with dead-set resolution. "Promise me."

"What are you going to do? Jump off the Stratocaster?"

I point at the building—the one that's even taller than the Space Needle—at the far end of the Strip. "Because there's no way I'm doing that with you. Friendship only goes so far."

"I'm not jumping." Jazz motions for us to turn onto a gritty little side street. I follow, making sure Macie's hand is held tightly in mine. "I'm going to get a tattoo."

In the time it takes me to recover from my shock, Jazz has led the way into a tiny little tattoo parlor, where a guy with painfully large gauges in his ears greets us with a missing-toothed grin. "Ready to get inked?"

Macie and I shake our heads back and forth like we're on fast-forward, but Jazz squares her shoulders and nods.

"Jazz, what are you doing?" I hiss the words under my breath. "You know this is going to be permanent, right?"

"If I wanted it to wash right off, I would've gone to one of the henna places on Front Street ages ago." The words escape from between Jazz's tightly clenched teeth. "I have to do this."

"You...do?" I shake my head. "What are you going to get?"

A wry smile slips onto Jazz's face, but it wobbles a bit. "You'll see."

Two hours later, we emerge from the tattoo parlor, Jazz sporting a freshly inked "cut below dotted line" tattoo on her stump and me and Macie both mercifully ink-free. Jazz is grinning like she won the lottery—which I guess she sort of did.

"I don't get it." Macie trots along after us as we set off in the direction of the MGM Grand Casino. Midori got us tickets to her favorite magic show, and we'll miss it if we don't hurry up.

"It's a joke." Jazz raises her hands, as if in exasperation, then points to the dotted line circling her stump. "You know—how you're supposed to cut below the dotted line? I want it to look like that's what the doctors did to me."

Macie groans and rolls her eyes, like Jazz's explanation is the epitome of bad comedy. "Why did you waste all your money on *that*? If I was going to get a tattoo, I'd get a piece of cake stamped right over my heart."

I snicker since Macie is kidding—at least I hope she is—but Jazz's mouth is set in a hard, sober line. "I did it because I had to. I needed to do something to show everyone that...my stump...that this is *me*. I am who I am. I'm different, and that's okay. I'd rather have random people at the grocery stare at my stump and laugh than get all awkward about it."

"But everyone knows you've only got one leg. It's who you are. That's one of the reasons why Dani loves having you at the rescue place, right?"

"So the kids can relate to me." Jazz lifts her chin. "Fine, then. Maybe it's not so much me needing to show other people that my stump is who I am. Maybe it's...I don't know. I just needed to do it is all."

"It's okay. You don't have to explain it to us." But, in the silence that hangs between our words, Jazz's real answer comes forth whether she knows it or not.

This tattoo is about more than Jazz helping others realize that's she's proud of the person she is. It's not a cheap joke or conversation starter. It's Jazz who really needs this tattoo—not just to bring a smile to her face but also to help her love herself for who she is. Missing leg and all.

And I sure hope it works, because I know I love her to death…and I think someone else is pretty smitten with her too.

# Chapter Twenty-Two

"OLIVE!" IF HE WASN'T SO HAPPY to see me, I'd think Brander was seriously trying to hurt me when he bowls me over with a hug at the airport on Monday afternoon. "Man, I missed you." He whispers the words into my hair, following them with a kiss to my cheek before offering Jazz and Macie more reserved versions of his tackle hug.

He grills us about Las Vegas the whole way home, until he drops Jazz and Macie off at the doggie rescue to make the evening feeding rounds.

"Can I spend the night?" Macie calls over her shoulder as she hops out of the car. "I have everything I need in my suitcase!"

I shrug. "If Jazz says it's okay. Call Gramma though, to be sure."

Macie shoots me a thumbs-up and snatches her bag from the trunk before jogging inside, yelling after Jazz. How anyone could have enough energy to spend the night dealing with a houseful of dogs after the trip we had, I don't even know.

"Sounds like quite the weekend." Brander pulls away from the curb, slipping his hand into mine as he turns toward Gramma's house. "You must be exhausted."

"Sort of. But I slept most of the way home."

"You did, huh?" He peeks over at me. "In that case...you wouldn't happen to be hungry, would you?"

"Only a little bit." I hold up my fingers, pinched together.

"All they had on the plane was flat soda."

"Phew." Brander runs a hand against his forehead. "Good thing I thought to make a reservation at the Lahaina Grill."

"You didn't dare." I swat Brander's arm. The Lahaina Grill was the site of our first "real date," and we've never darkened the overly posh restaurant's doorstep since.

"No, but I do have a table booked at Aloha Mixed Plate. You don't know anyone who would want to join me, do you?"

"I can't think of anything I'd like more." I relax against the smooth leather seat, but I barely get comfortable before something hits me smack in the chest.

Between Brander's bachelor trip and my visit to Vegas, I haven't had a chance to break the news to Brander. In fact, I'd nearly allowed myself to forget about it.

*The Shave Ice Shack is closing.*

Those words become a refrain, pulsing in my ears and ringing in my chest for the rest of the drive. They're quelled slightly by the golden-hour sunlight and vintage reggae tunes surrounding the tables at Aloha Mixed Plate, but they pick up again as soon as we order.

"You're sure you're not tired?" Brander casts a glance my way in between snapping pictures of the sunset. You'd think that, after living on the island since he was born, Brander would be tired of the ocean view by now—but he never seems to be. One look at Anchor's social media pages makes that perfectly clear.

"Olive? Did I lose you?" Brander waves a hand in front of my face. "You're awfully quiet. Did something happen in Vegas?"

"Not Vegas, no." I shake my head. "But before. Brander, it—it's not good news."

His forehead pinches. "Are you okay? Are *we* okay?"

"Of course. But I *do* have something to tell you—and you have to promise to keep it confidential."

"Olive, please tell me what's wrong."

"The Shave Ice Shack is closing."

"*What?*" Good thing I told Brander before we got our food, or he totally would've choked on his poi. "No way. Are you sure? How do you know?"

"Straight from the horse's mouth." I give him the un-sweetened- condensed version of my upcoming article for the *West Maui Sun.*

By the time I'm done, the sun is nearly to the horizon, but even with its pink-and-gold rays stretching across the bay to light our table, I don't have the heart to pay it any mind. Brander seems shaken too, his usually omnipresent smile compressed into a tight line across his stubbled face. "And he said he won't sell out?"

"He said something about it being a good run, but that all runs have to end sometime. I think he hates the thought of someone buying the place out and turning it into a tourist trap."

"That makes sense." And then, like someone flips a switch, Brander ducks his head and pulls out his phone, typing furiously for several moments.

"Sorry." He looks up sheepishly and slides the phone into his pants pocket. "I had to send an email. For—for work. I forgot about it until you said that thing about tourist traps."

*Work.*

The word lodges in my craw like an oversized lemon—pith and all. "Is this how it's always going to be?"

"What do you mean?"

"Us passing each other like ships in the night until we can finally get together for a date? And then, when we do, you still working?" The words come out stronger than I'd planned, and I regret them a little once I've said them. But not enough. "I know your job is important to your dad, but half the time I feel like it's running your life. Is it that important to *you*?"

"Olive, I'm sorry...I—"

"Forget it." I shake my head, cheeks already starting to burn. "I'm tired. I don't know what I'm saying. If you like your job, that's fine. But if you don't...well, then I don't know what to say."

Brander opens his mouth. Closes it. Then opens it again.

But before he can say anything, a waitress with a flower in her hair stops at our table to deposit two plates loaded with kalua pork and imu-roasted beef. As soon as she leaves, Brander reaches across the table for my hand. "Let's pray."

And so we do, first Brander, then myself. His part of the prayer is short—simple—but mine is longer. Before I know it, I'm pouring out my heart to both Brander and God, my jumbled thoughts running out in a crazy, twisted ribbon that I don't hardly expect—or even need—them to know what to do with.

Because sometimes all a person needs is to be *heard.*

"The Shave Ice Shack is closing! Can you even believe it?" Jazz practically shrieks in my ear through the phone when she calls on Friday. *Oops.*

I let the whole story spill then and saying it all over again makes it even worse. "I'm sorry, Jazz. I should've told you sooner, but I didn't want to ruin our trip."

"At least I had a trusty informant."

"Who, Brander?"

"Hunter."

"You guys are still talking?"

"Well, *excuse* me. I didn't think it was against the law." Jazz snorts, but I can tell from the sound of her voice that she's smiling. "Besides, Hunter and I are taking part in this pretty big ceremony called a *wedding*—maybe you've heard of it. If we don't coordinate the—stuff—then who will?"

"What *stuff?*"

"None of your beeswax."

"Oh."

"So, are we going or not?" Jazz asks after a beat of silence.

"Going where?"

"To the Shave Ice Shack! If it's going to close, I at least want to cash in the full punch cards I've been hoarding."

"Say no more."

By the time I arrive at the Shave Ice Shack—after changing into my weekend attire, saying hi-and-bye to Gramma, and assuring Macie that her latest sugar-laden creation looks better than something from a Martha Stewart magazine— Jazz is already there, as are the guys.

"I thought the wedding party could use some bonding time." Jazz smiles at me, but I don't think it's my imagination that her grin widens when she peeks over at Hunter. She must catch me watching, though, because she shoots me a glare that says *not a word.*

After we get our orders, Hunter pulls out his phone and twirls it around on the picnic table we snagged. "Should we show them or what?"

A flicker of excitement lights in my chest. "Show us what?"

"Hunter." Brander mock-groans and rests his head in his hands. "We weren't going to show them *now*. It's for the rehearsal!"

"No way, man. I can't wait that long."

"Go ahead then, now that you've spoiled the surprise." Brander shakes his head at Hunter, then at me. "Sorry, Olive."

Before I can reply, Hunter taps his phone a few times and music starts pouring out of it—really, really *good* music.

After an upbeat, ukulele-laden intro, Brander's voice comes on, singing words that are...just for me.

*It's a truth we all acknowledge,*
*That a young man wants a wife,*
*It'll be you and me, girl,*
*For the rest of my whole life.*

"He got that bit from *Pride and Prejudice*." Hunter jabs his thumb at Brander, then stares across the table at...Jazz. She turns her head, apparently oblivious. *Oh, brother.* How much longer are they going to keep up the charade?

Until a certain bouquet toss, perhaps?

The music keeps playing, swelling higher and higher into a chorus with a syncopated drum beat.

*Yeah, it's just you and me girl,*
*Weathering the storm,*
*Even when this life is crazy,*
*It's your love that keeps me warm.*

"Dude, this thing is sappy." Jazz shakes her head at

Brander before her eyes flit over to Hunter. There's no time to psychoanalyze the movement though, because Brander's voice starts in on the second verse.

*Sometimes the world seems crazy,*
*Like problems never end,*
*But does it really matter,*
*When I'm in love with my best friend?*

I blink, a sudden mist pooling in my eyes, as Brander repeats the chorus in preparation for the bridge.

*Heart to heart,*
*Hand in hand,*
*On His rock,*
*Our love will stand.*

"Oh, it will stand..." Hunter croons along with the track under his breath, tapping his fingers in time with the prerecorded beat. I'd kill to hear them play this song live.

By the time the last chord sounds, my eyes are more than misty. Brander's grinning so wide I'm afraid his mouth will never close again. "Do you like it?"

"I love it. It's...wow." I sniff, then clear my throat. "Sorry. I guess I'm..."

"Don't be sorry." Brander stands and rounds the table to rest his hands on my shoulders. "It was kinda supposed to make you cry."

"You're mean." I pretend to slap him across the arm, then pull him down and plant a kiss squarely on his jaw. "But I don't mind that."

And then, as he pulls me into a tight embrace, an idea lights in my mind. So impossible—so *wonderfully* impossible—that it might actually work. I pull away and lean across the table, doing my best to hide the sneaky smile threatening to spill across my face.

"Hunter, could you send me a copy of that song?"

It doesn't take long that evening for me to find exactly what I'm looking for—a small, grassroots record label right here on Maui. One that has helped launch a handful of local celebrities and even a couple of national sensations. I'm no talent scout, but I email them the song and a link to the band's website anyway, crossing my fingers as the attachment uploads. *God, I think this is what You want. If not, then fine. But I have to try. For Brander. For Hunter. For all of us.*

"For all of who?" Gramma's voice nearly startles me straight off the porch swing.

"How long have you been out here?" *And how much of that prayer did I say out loud?*

"What kind of scheme do you have going on now?"

"One that should probably be kept under wraps unless it actually pans out. But since you're here..." I pat the bench for Gramma to sit, then pull up the online wedding inspiration board that Midori added me to. "You could help me with something else."

"What's that?" Gramma bites her lip, as if nervous, but she takes a seat next to me anyway. "Midori's already got me running all over kingdom-come, trying to figure out how Macie and I can make enough treats for a whole dessert bar. My goodness, things were so much simpler when I was young."

"I know, Grams. But I think you'll like this—see?" I point to the photos I've pinned, all different ways to honor Mom at the wedding. "I want to do something special—to make sure she's still *there* as much as she can be."

"Oh." Gramma leans in for a closer look. "*Oh.*"

I point to a picture of a space on a church pew next to that of the father of the bride. It's empty, reserved for the bride's mom, except...it's not. "We could take pieces of lace from Mom's wedding dress and get a picture of her to put on the chair next to you and Dad and Emily. Or what about this?" I point to a different picture where a bride and groom are about to release a balloon bouquet in honor of lost loved ones.

"Olive..." Gramma's usual warm, strong gaze wavers as she turns to me. "These are beautiful. Especially since—"

"Since what?"

"Nothing." She shakes her head, the saggy bit of skin under her chin quivering.

"You're thinking about Dad and Emily, aren't you?"

"It's foolish of me. Yes, I want Alex to move on and be happy, but...imagining him with someone other than Sophie..."

"Oh, Grams." This time, I'm the one to wrap my arms around her. Her shoulders shake as I hold her tighter...tighter...

"Olive, dear." Her voice is choked. "I can't breathe."

"Oops, sorry." I release my grip and lean back to study Gramma's face. Her eyes are bright, but she's smiling. "So, should we do it?"

"Yes." She nods. "Absolutely."

We get to work and stay that way for an hour, Gramma sketching sample designs for the chair's decor until the light fades so completely from the sky that we can barely see.

"Mom would love it." I wrap my arm around Gramma and lean against her shoulder, staring out into the black-velvet night surrounding us. The streetlight across the road is burnt out, but I can still see the crest and crash of each wave thanks to a silvery strand of moonlight.

Gramma sighs, her breath coming out in one long, low stream. "You know, there isn't a day that's gone by since that ring went on your finger that I don't find myself wishing Sophie could see the beautiful young woman you've become."

My throat grows thick. "If only she could've met Brander. Hear him sing." I rest my head in my hands. "I wish she could help me and Jazz and Macie get ready. Take a million pictures and embarrass me. Dance with Dad at the reception." Uh-oh. Rambling. Not good. *Rein it in, Olive. Rein it in.*

Too late.

One tear. Two tears. Three. "I wish life was *fair* and that I still had a mom and Jazz's mom had gotten better after rehab and Macie didn't have to grow up and…you know."

"I do." Gramma lays one hand on my knee, her usual grandmotherly strength seemingly restored. "I also know it's getting late. Go get some sleep, and we'll talk again later."

I open my mouth to protest. What good is sleep when I need help? But there's a devious spark in Gramma's eyes, one that usually hints that she knows more than she's letting on.

Maybe something like…another letter.

# Chapter Twenty-Three

As it turns out, that letter is a long, long time in coming. When it finally arrives on a slightly drizzly Sunday morning, I tear into it like a starving surfer dude would tear into an extra-large Pirate Pete's pizza. Foregoing breakfast for a chance to spend a few minutes alone with Mom before church, I head out to the front porch and sit on the swing before reading.

*One month to go!*

*Hello, my sweet girl. The wedding is coming up soon, and you might be feeling a little stressed and overwhelmed. It might seem as if nothing is coming together the way it's supposed to, but don't worry. God has everything under control, and rest assured that I'm standing right up there with Him, keeping watch over you. I love you, baby girl. Now and forever.*

The usual lump that comes from reading one of Mom's notes sticks squarely in my throat, but I swallow hard against it and push the letter into its wax-sealed envelope. *One month to go.* It seems too long and, at the same time, *way* too short.

Midori must be thinking the same thing, because I get a text form her when we're halfway to church: **Would you and the rest of your entourage like to meet this afternoon to go over final details?**

I relay the message to Grams and Macie, both of whom agree, though Macie's assent is considerably less-than-enthusiastic.

"What's wrong, Mace? Aren't you excited?"

"Excited to get this thing over with. You're so *boring* when you have a bridezilla brain."

"Hey! If anyone's a bridezilla, it's Midori."

"Yeah, right." I don't need to turn around in my seat up front next to Gramma to tell that Macie is rolling her eyes. With gusto. "You're obsessed, and I'm sick of it. I'd rather stay after church and scrape sand off the floor than watch Jazz try out one more hairstyle on you. Get over yourself."

"Macie!" Gramma's voice is stern, though not as terse as my own tone would be. Maybe she's thinking about her own sister-of-the-bride experience. "This wedding is a very special day for Olive—and for you. Don't forget that you're going to get all dressed up too."

"Yeah, Mace. It'll be fun."

"The only *fun* thing about it will be when it's over." Macie snorts, and I have half a mind to crawl into the backseat and tickle a better response out of her, but I know it wouldn't work. Macie isn't the same little girl who could be talked out of a bad mood with nothing more than the promise of a sweet treat or movie night. She's growing up—and so am I.

But even though a lot in our lives is changing, our relationship doesn't have to.

"Why'd I let you talk me into this? I could be hanging out with Kanani right now." Macie mumbles the words, stabbing at a blanched spear of asparagus in her otherwise-empty bowl. "Besides, this food is totally gross. Shouldn't it be a sin for Christians to eat anything called a buddha bowl?"

I snort, and Jazz joins in from her spot across the table. Thankfully, Midori is running around inside trying to find her massive wedding-planning portfolio and Brander and August are—you guessed it—burning the midnight oil down at the office, so Gramma is the only other one within ear-shot.

"Macie, get your attitude together. Midori was very kind to have us over for lunch, and you should be grateful." So says Gramma, who's currently trying to hide a mountain of quinoa under a wilted spinach leaf. Health food and my family definitely don't mix.

I catch Jazz's eye and we share a snicker as Midori staggers outside, juggling her massive stack of wedding-planning resources. "Here we go." She sets the whole pile on the table with a mighty *thunk*, then reaches across to hand me an embossed sheet of paper. "The wedding programs came in yesterday. I think they turned out splendidly."

And they did—the paper is thick and creamy, and Brander's and my names are embossed in shimmery rose-gold foil—but...

"This is wrong." Jazz points to a line of text on my program and frowns.

"What do you mean?" Midori squints at me. "They say—"

"This is for an *Olivia* and Brander. Autocorrect—it gets you every time. Better call the company and tell them they made a mistake."

"Mistake?" Midori rises from her seat at the table and clack-clacks over to me, her spiky stiletto heels beating a death march against the patio. My gut clenches as I stare at my own copy of the program.

Mistake, my foot. What should I expect after all those

times I never bothered to set Midori straight when she called me Olivia?

Jazz snatches the program out of my hands. "Yep, it's a mistake all right. Midori, I hope you can get a refund. And a rush-order." She hands the sheet to Gramma. "Take a look, *Tutu.*"

"But what's *wrong* with them? Is it the style?" Midori chews on her lip. "I researched eighteenth-century typography to find something with that cottage-core aesthetic that's so popular. If you'd prefer something more modern, I suppose—"

"No, Midori. The fonts are great. It looks like something out of a Jane Austen novel." A lump appears in my throat, and everything in my stomach that *was* in that buddha bowl threatens to jump right back into it. "It's my fault."

"I still don't understand what's wrong." Midori's pointy-toed slingback shoe hammers the tiled patio like a jackhammer. Not good.

"It's my name." My cheeks flush with heat. "My name is Olive—it's not a nickname. My mom wanted to name me Olivia, but when I was born my eyes were so green that Dad convinced her to change my name to Olive. Seriously—it's on my birth certificate." My cheeks warm at the semi-embarrassing bit of family lore. Why couldn't I have been named after a great-aunt—or anything other than my eye color and one of Mom's go-to pregnancy cravings?

But of course, we have bigger problems now.

Namely how I'm going to get through the ceremony without cringing or crying at the thought of having the name *Olivia* emblazoned across every single wedding program. Mom was the only one who ever called me that when she was feeling spunky—to give Dad a hard time.

Midori paces the terrace, phone already pressed to her ear—like customer service is going to be working on a Sunday?

My stomach churns, and someone—Jazz—takes my hand as Midori leaves a long, rambling message.

"Olive, why didn't you correct me when I used the wrong name? Why didn't *any* of you? I feel like a fool." Midori's cheeks are ruby-red as she pockets her phone. "It's a simple enough mistake, after all."

"One people have made dozens of times. I'm sorry." Suddenly my eyes feel a bit too moist. I push away from the table and take a few faltering steps toward Midori, then stop. "I'm sorry," I say again, though the words feel feeble. "I don't know why I didn't say anything. I guess part of me was embarrassed. Another part...well, my mom used to call me Olivia sometimes."

"Oh." Midori wrings her hands. "I still shouldn't have..."

"I like them." Gramma speaks up from her spot at the table and lays the program alongside her plate. "If Sophie was here, she'd be getting a real chuckle out of this. Olive is right, after all—Sophie never wanted to change the name in the first place."

"But, but—"

"I'll tell you what." I cross over to Midori and sling my arm around her petite shoulders. "Gramma's right. We can keep the programs. It'll be a great conversation starter."

"No, dear. I don't want it to ruin your perfect day."

"It won't."

"But how can I make it up to you?"

"There's nothing you need to—wait a minute. There is something, after all. I want your mom at the wedding. Sitting right up front."

Midori's posture stiffens beneath my arm. "But they're *wrong.* And my mother..."

"Isn't perfect either. But I still love her." I clasp my free hand to my chest, practically begging. "Please, Midori. She should be there."

And then, it's as if a huge weight drops from Midori's shoulders. Her rigid stance melts away like a shave ice in the bright sunshine, and she bows her head. "She will be."

# Chapter Twenty-Four

"GALLOWAY?" MARK'S VOICE IS GRUFF WHEN he pops into my office cubicle a couple of weeks later. Gruffer than usual, I should say. "You're off the case."

"What?" I lift my eyes from my computer and stare at him, commas and semicolons clouding my vision.

"The article. Forget about it."

"Which article? The one on the effects of sales tax on the tourism industry?" *Phew.*

"No. The Shave Ice Shack exclusive. Send me the notes that you got at that interview and everything else you've done."

"Wait, the Shave Ice Shack story?" The one I've been pouring my heart and soul into? "But it's almost all written. The deadline is tomorrow!"

"Tough luck, Galloway. Send me what you have. I'll take it from here."

"But—"

"What, do you have a problem with that?" He grunts. "Seems like you'd have more of a problem with losing your job. Send me the article, Galloway. Now."

Mark turns and disappears through the door before I can argue—and how can I? I sure don't feel like losing my job right before my wedding. Even still...

Tears fill my eyes as I open an email document and upload my files. Mark only cares about flashy headlines and getting new readers. But a story like this, one that—at its core—is a decades-long love story, needs heart. *Soul.* Definitely not a cheap title and cheesy spin.

Hank and his wife deserve better than that.

I press send on the email, and my heart breaks a little even as the gears in my head start turning. If I can't write Hank Murphy and his wife the story they deserve, then there has to be something else I can do for them during their last month of business—but what?

"Have them cater the wedding." Jazz's voice is so matter of fact when I tell her the whole story that I'm surprised I didn't think of it myself. "If Tutu's getting stressed about Midori's dessert bar idea, why not have the Shave Ice Shack come in and give out shave ice? With bottomless refills of course."

"Jazz, you're a genius!" I shriek and jump up from Jazz's bed with such a clatter that several dogs in the next room over start yipping and yapping.

"I *am* pretty brilliant." She mock bows and brushes her free-flowing hair over one shoulder. "Thanks for finally noticing."

"I've always known it. I bet Hunter has too." I waggle my eyebrows at Jazz. "What ever happened with him and Breeze, huh? He's never mentioned a dog."

"Nah." Jazz's fingers whip through her mane, turning it into a perfectly plaited braid right before my eyes. The girl seriously missed her calling as a hairdresser. "Hunter decided a cat would be more Breeze's speed."

"A cat? You mean like...*oh.*" Something in my chest falls a little bit. That prickly little ball of fluff with eyes so much like Mom's has been absent the last few times I've been over to the rescue, which must mean... "Did Breeze adopt that kitten that's been hanging around?"

Jazz bites her lip, then opens her mouth. Before she can answer, her phone buzzes, effectively cutting her off. "I'd better get that." She digs into her shorts pocket, answers the call, and puts it on speaker.

"We have a problem." Hunter's voice sounds tinny coming out of Jazz's phone in the middle of the small bedroom.

"What's that?" Jazz leans toward the phone.

"Hank just sent a blast email to all of his employees. Today's the Shave Ice Shack's last day in business."

"What?" My heart gives a sudden kick. "No way. Hank said they weren't going to close until the end of the month."

"This calls for a last hurrah, don't you think? Wanna get a shave ice after youth group? Brander and I are playing tonight."

*Hopefully this time he shows up.* I don't have time to voice that thought before Jazz jumps in. "I'll have both pockets loaded. If this is my last chance for an ice, I'm gonna go all out."

"Me too." The words seem to echo in Jazz's tiny room, reverberating in my ears. If Hank is closing up shop today, that must mean his wife took a turn for the worse. And if that's true, then Jazz's bright idea is too little too late.

"Sold out. Sold *out* of shave ice." Hunter shakes his head and his messy bun comes loose, sending renegade ringlets spilling down his neck. "How is that even possible?"

"I've seen it happen before." Brander lifts his hands. "But yeah, it totally stinks."

"Well, we have to get *something* to eat." Jazz lays one hand over her stomach. "I'm starving."

"Half the kalua pig wasn't enough?" Hunter slaps her on the back, but his hand stays there a little longer than it would if he was only teasing her.

Jazz shakes her head. "Not even close. Wanna head up to Ono Gelato?"

Brander shrugs. "Olive?"

"I've never been, but if you guys like it…"

"Wait…" Brander does a double take "You've never been?"

"I wasn't born with my toes in the sand like you guys. What, am I missing something?"

Brander shakes his head, his cowlick flopping over into his eyes. "What am I going to do with you? Come on." He tugs on my hand and leads me along the beachside path, all the way to the Whaler's Village shopping center. Once we're there, Jazz and Hunter practically race each other to be first in line at the gelato counter.

"What flavor should I get?" I stare at a case with two dozen flavors, a colorful kaleidoscope of sugar and cream and…*yum.* "They all look so good."

"Want me to order you my favorite?" Brander leans close to whisper, his breath tickling my ear and sending a shiver down my spine.

Before I know it, we're all wandering along the beach, each clutching a double-scoop cone. "What flavor *is* this thing?" I peer down at it in the twilight.

"Sandy beach. Try it—you'll see. It has graham crackers for the sand."

I do as I'm told, licking…swallowing… "Yuck." I wrinkle my nose and jerk the cone away. "It's all…peanut-y."

"And that's a bad thing?" Jazz doesn't stop slurping on her own cone.

"Um, yeah." I wrinkle my nose. Brander might as well have ordered me a deviled-egg-flavored scoop. "Peanut butter and I don't mix."

"You're not, like, going to have an allergic reaction, are you?" Hunter bites his lip, letting a huge drip from his own cone run all the way down his arm to his elbow.

"No, nothing like that. Here—" I hand the rest of it to Brander, who's already halfway done with his own cone. "You finish it."

"Gosh, Brander, didn't you learn anything in premarital counseling?" Jazz turns to give him the stink eye.

Brander laughs, one cone in each hand. "Yeah, we did. But not stuff like that."

"You didn't even talk about your pet peeves?"

Brander and I shake our heads, nearly in unison. "We still have one meeting left, though. Maybe we'll get to those then. Right?" I peer at Brander.

"Right." He nods, and with that motion, a spark of electricity shoots through my stomach. Like it or not, I have a feeling this last premarital counseling session is going to be a big one.

"One week." Brander's fingers intertwine with my own as we walk along the beach to our arranged meeting spot with Jonah at Whaler's Village.

"Seven days." I stare up at Brander, unable to keep from beaming at him. Who cares if I've got a chronic case of tourist-style honeymoon eyes? In seven short days, Brander and I will say our I-do's and share our first kiss as man and wife. It's...

"Crazy." Brander shakes his head, somehow managing

to finish my sentence even though I didn't speak it out loud. "Wasn't it, like, last week that you told me off in my own front yard?"

"That was only because that dumb dog of yours tried to eat my kneecap." I cross my arms with a pretend huff. "Seems like it was last week that you took me out to dinner to grill me about my 'mental and spiritual well-being'."

"Aw, man." Brander slaps a hand to his forehead. "I was so smooth."

"The smoothest."

Sharing a laugh, we stroll past the cabana-style shops that mark the entrance to the resort shopping district. Brander is still chuckling under his breath by the time we meet Jonah in front of a hopping open-air restaurant in the middle of the complex.

We make small talk while we wait for a table and place our orders, but the second our waitress disappears, Jonah is all business. "How are you guys? Nervous? Excited? Getting cold feet?"

"No cold feet here." Brander's flip-flop nudges my own beneath the table. "What about you, Olive?"

I shake my head. "Nope. I was wondering though—when exactly are we going to get to the important stuff here? We've talked about budgeting and kids and all that, but what about day-to-day life? I'm telling you right now that I don't like the idea of falling into the toilet in the middle of the night because *someone* forgot to put the seat down."

"Hey! My mom raised me better than that."

"Phew." I wipe an imaginary bead of sweat from my forehead and take a sip of water before turning to Jonah. "For real though, I've never shared a house with anyone other than my family. I've never even lived alone. What happens when Brander and I get over our newlywed bliss and start nit-picking each other?"

"That's exactly what we're going to talk about." Jonah spreads open his Bible. "You know, everything you hear about the honeymoon phase is a lie, right?"

Brander cocks his head at Jonah. "Are you saying we won't always feel this in love?"

"I didn't say that." Jonah holds up both hands, like he's trying to stop a stampede of questions. "The Bible tells us that a man who finds a wife has found a very good thing indeed. Marriage is a great blessing. But even the best blessings in the world have their downsides. People annoy each other—that's a fact of life. Why do you think couples end up getting divorced?"

Brander chews on his bottom lip, like he's thinking hard about the question, but his answer is a simple one. "Because they don't have God in the middle."

"Exactly. Even if I gave you a ten-page-long questionnaire to help diagnose the potential problem areas of everyday life, I wouldn't be able to cover everything. Instead, I'm going to give you a comprehensive guide to handling anything that might arise in the next...oh, sixty years or so."

"You mean prayer?" I reach under the table for Brander's hand. "Don't worry—we already do that. Both alone *and* as a couple."

"Actually, no. That's what most couples think I'm getting at, but I'm talking about something even deeper. I'm talking about *love.*"

"But...you're making it sound like all the lovey-dovey wears off with the honeymoon phase." I squint at Jonah.

"Not so fast." Jonah holds up a finger. "I'm talking about true love—the kind that never leaves. But there's a difference. The feeling of being 'in love?' That'll disappear the first time you fall into that toilet bowl."

I shudder at the thought.

"Being *in love* is great, but *true love* is a choice. It's not something we fall into or feel—it's something we walk into boldly, knowing that we've made the decision to lay our life down to better serve our beloved. Are you ready to make that commitment?"

"Yes." Brander and I speak together, and he gives my hand a squeeze beneath the table as our waitress reappears, toting plates piled with burgers and fries. I watch him out of the corner of my eye as the waitress distributes our food. The slight twinkle in his gaze, the jaunty twist of his cowlick, the warm smile on his face...

A thrill flies through my chest, accentuated by the warm rays of afternoon sunshine falling across my face.

*One week.*

The voice whispering in my head sounds suspiciously like Mom's, and I cling to it, let it repeat itself over and over again in my head until its words stays there as Jonah bows his to offer up a prayer.

We're quiet for a few moments as we eat, but inside, my mind is racing.

One week until the wedding—until I marry my very best friend. One week until I say a different sort of goodbye. Not a painful one, necessarily, but one that will come with a few tears, nonetheless. I'll say goodbye to Gramma's house, to sharing a room with Macie...to the last vestiges of my childhood.

But—and my heart swells at the thought—I'll be saying hello. Hello to a new life and a new house. Hello to mornings spent with the man that I love. Hello to everything else that God has in store.

But, before I get to that point, I'll have to make it through the wedding.

# Chapter Twenty-Five

MY PHONE BUZZES IN MY POCKET as Brander, Jonah, and I leave the restaurant later that night, each of us toting to-go boxes filled with massive slices of the eatery's famous banana cream pie.

"Hang on a sec, you guys." I plop onto a bench before pulling out my phone. My wedding gift to Brander—an engraved guitar pick—was due to come in the mail today, and I made Grams promise to call me when it came.

But it's not Gramma. It's not even a number I recognize. I stare at the phone as it rings...

Rings...

"Hello?" I answer at the last second.

"Brander Delacroix?" The man's voice is worn and gravely, but there's something in it that sparks with excitement. "Is this a good time?"

"Um, this isn't Brander. It's his fiancée, Olive."

"Olive? Hmm. Did you send me the email, then?"

"What email? Who is this?" I grip the phone tighter. It couldn't be—could it?

"This is Stan Wallace, from Paʻipaʻi Lima Studios. You sent us an email with a demo tape from Brander's band." The voice sounds frustrated, as if the answer should be obvious. And maybe it is, but it also seems too good to be true.

"What did you think?"

"We want to sign him."

I drop the phone from my face, my mouth falling open

despite any effort to maintain my composure. Gramma's words from that night return to me. *God works all things for good.*

And this—this is definitely *good.*

"Hello? *Hello?*" Stan's voice booms from the phone. "Is this some sort of joke?"

"No, sir." I'm quick to return the phone to my face. "Not a joke. Do you want to talk to him?"

"Yes." The guy makes a noise that could be a either laugh or a huff. "That's exactly what I want."

Everything fast-forwards after that, and suddenly the phone is in Brander's hands and he's grinning and nodding. Jonah keeps looking from me to Brander and back again. Then suddenly Brander is hanging up and running toward me and then—*oof*—he's hugging me so tight he squeezes all of the air right out of my chest.

"Thank you." Brander plants a kiss on my jaw, then another right on my lips. I kiss him back—longer and harder than I usually would, because this is *big.* Huge.

This is...*this is all You, God.*

The excitement has barely died down by the time Brander and I say goodbye to Jonah and drive down the highway over our condo.

"I still don't get why we need to bother stopping." I hoist my takeout box in the air as Brander whips around a curve, his usual dedication to staying under the posted speed limit obviously forgotten in his excitement. "We should head to the beach and celebrate." *In other words, dig into this pie.*

"I know, but my mom's been checking up on the condo every week to make sure everything's ship-shape. She's so busy with final prep that I figured it was the least we could do."

"Why? It's not like this place is a squatter magnet or anything."

"You know my mom."

"Fine, but let's make it quick—we have a record deal to celebrate."

When Brander unlocks the door to our condo, bright light spills out from the doorway, as well the pounding beat of music from Brander's favorite vintage rock station. I peek at Brander. "You wouldn't happen to know anything about this, would you?"

He raises his hands. "At least these squatters have good taste, huh?"

Jazz and Macie tackle me when I step inside. "You took *forever!*" Macie mock-glares at me. "Brander said you guys would be done at eight."

"Sorry, Mace." Brander doesn't look too sorry. "Something...came up."

"Uh-oh." Jazz's eyes widen. "Did Jonah try to scare you off at the last session?"

"No, nothing like that. Brander, do you want to tell them?"

"Tell us what?" Hunter pushes between Jazz and Macie. Grams, August, and Midori are close behind. "Dude, what happened? You look like you won the lottery."

"Nah." Brander shakes his head. "But *we* did."

"What's all this about?" Gramma cocks her head at us.

"We'll tell you in a minute. Let's all go sit in the living room."

It takes more than a minute for all of us to get settled in the small, cozy living room, but we eventually manage. Macie replaces Brander's and my takeout boxes with hot, gooey macadamia-nut brownies and plants herself right in front of us with an expectant look on her face. "You have to at least take a *bite* before you start talking. Otherwise they'll get cold."

Brander and I do as we're told, leaning up against the chair Gramma's claimed as her own, but Jazz's jiggling knee and Hunter's expectant expression keep me from reveling in chocolate heaven for too long. "Brander, are you going to tell them or should I?"

"Let's do it together." He reaches over and grabs my hand. "Ready? On the count of three..."

Jazz, Hunter, and the others do a fine job of counting us off, and then Brander and I yell at the top of our lungs— "Anchor got a record deal!"

For a moment, the silence is staggering as Jazz and Hunter's mouths fall in unison. Even Midori looks appropriately surprised. Then Hunter springs up off the couch and nearly takes Brander to the ground with his hug. "Dude!" He's practically shaking when he pulls away. "How? I thought—"

"Don't get too excited." I wave a finger in the air and mumble the words around a mouthful of my brownie. "You're not going to Nashville or anything."

"It's a smaller label based here in Hawaii. Check it out." Brander pulls up the company's website and hands his phone to Hunter. "He said he'd send the contract over later this week."

"Dude." Hunter shakes his head and scrolls down the page. "How'd you find them? Why didn't you tell me?"

"It was all Olive." Brander takes my hand. "She sent in that song—the one we were supposed to play at the rehearsal dinner."

"Then I guess you *should* be thanking me." Hunter winks. "If I hadn't spoiled the surprise, then Olive never would've had a demo song to send them."

Brander shakes his head. "At least there's one surprise you didn't manage to spoil. Olive?" He helps me up from the floor.

Jazz snorts. "The only reason he didn't spoil that surprise is because he didn't *know* about it."

"Know about what?" Hunter glances over as Brander leads me to the bedroom.

"Um, Brander..." I bite my lip and look at him.

"Open it." He waves a hand at the door. "There's something inside for you."

"You know, you've done weird stuff before, but this is a whole new level."

"Just open the door."

I do as he tells me, step inside, and...

*Pounce.*

Something furry and fluffy and tiger-striped lands right on top of my bare foot, then stares up at me with those eyes that could've belonged to Mom. "Mango?" I squat to pat the cat's oversized ears, then look up at Brander. "I thought Breeze adopted her. Jazz said..."

"All I said was that Breeze got a cat. But her family took her to the Lanai Cat Sanctuary to get one." Jazz joins us in the doorway. "Mango was yours from the minute you rescued her."

"You mean..."

Brander points to the bed, where half a dozen cat toys

are arranged, along with a hand-lettered sign—*A house is not a home unless it has a cat.* "That goes for condos too, I hear." He looks even happier now than he did when he first heard about the record deal.

Sudden tears flood my eyes as I pick up the cat and nestle her in my arms. The ball of fluff nuzzles the crook of my arm, and her rumble-motor purr vibrates against my chest. Then, like a moment from one of those tearjerker pet movies Gramma always watches, the cat stares up at me with big blue eyes and meows and...

Suddenly it's like Mom is here with me too.

"Jazz, was this your idea?"

She lifts her chin. "I figured this was a way better wedding gift than something practical, like cleaning supplies."

I open my mouth to agree that yes, cats top toilet plungers any day of the week, when Midori sweeps into the room, her face ghostly white, August close on her heels.

"*Okaasan.*" Brander whirls around. "What's wrong?"

"I got a call. My mother—she's had a stroke."

# Chapter Twenty-Six

MIDORI WHITE-KNUCKLES THE CAR DOOR handle the entire way to Kahului, as if she's ready to jump out at a moment's notice, and her expression is different than it was the last time we drove this road together. Maybe it's because Gramma's station wagon—the only rig big enough to fit all of us—smells a little bit like wet dog, or maybe because this time she isn't simply dreading the visit. In fact, I'd wager a guess that Midori is terrified.

"I should have visited more often." She shakes her head, silky ebony hair falling from her perfectly styled French twist. "What if she's gone before we get there? What if I never get to say goodbye?"

My stomach clenches tighter and tighter. What do I do with the version of Midori sitting next to me? The calm, confident, capable woman is gone, replaced by a small, timid girl afraid of losing her mother.

A girl who, not all that long ago, could have been me.

"Don't worry." The words feel weird coming out of my mouth, and I know they're flimsy compared to the weight of the situation, but they're all I have to offer. "Your mom is a strong lady. She'll hang on."

"You think?" Midori peels her eyes from the road, fixing them instead on me.

"I *know*. God's got this all worked out. Trust me." Even though, inside, I'm not so sure I trust myself.

At exactly five minutes after midnight, Midori barges through the doors of the Maui Memorial Medical Center like a woman on a mission. The rest of us follow close behind. Except...

"Jazz?" I turn to find her standing stock still in the middle of the lobby. Her silvery-gray eyes are wide, and the usual tan on her face has faded to a ghostly white. "Are you okay?"

"I haven't been here since..." Her hand strays to her stump, where she traces the tattoo with one finger. "You know."

*Oh.*

"It's weird." She sniffs. "It still smells the same. Like..."

"Medicine?" Macie supplies, backtracking to join us.

Jazz shakes her head. "No. Sugarcoated suffering."

I flinch, and Macie does too.

"Sorry for being morbid, guys." Jazz ducks her head. "But this is weird."

"Jazz?" Flip-flopping footsteps sound behind me, and I turn to find Hunter trotting toward us. "What's the matter? Is it—*oh.*" He blinks at her scuffed metal prosthesis, as if seeing it for the first time.

"I haven't set foot in here—real *or* fake—since the amputation." Jazz's lip quivers. She turns to the side, and I move to give her a hug, but Hunter is too quick for me. Before I can reach Jazz, he's already wrapping his arms around her and holding tight.

I'm half expecting Jazz to struggle or resist his touch, but instead she relaxes into his hold, almost as if she's been waiting for it all along.

"Come on." I whisper the words and we both start after the others.

A last glance over my shoulder at Jazz and Hunter reveals that neither of them will be letting the other go any time soon.

*Obaasan* is resting comfortably by the time we get to her room, and so is Midori—curled up next to her mother in the hospital bed like she never wants to say goodbye again.

"Is she going to be okay?" I slip next to Brander and reach for his hand. It's cold—clammy.

He nods once. Barely. "It was a transient ischemic attack—a temporary blockage. She won't suffer any long-term side effects."

I take a deep breath of air, tinged with relief. "Your mom seems...okay?"

"Better than okay." Brander tugs on my hand to draw me closer to him, then wraps an arm around me. "I think this is what I've been praying for."

"What?" I nearly pull away, but Brander's hold on me is snug and secure—solid. Instead, I shoot him my best interpretation of the Hawaiian stink eye—with a bit of Boston sass thrown in for good measure. "I mean, you wanted your grandma to have a stroke?"

"No, not at all. But this is bringing them together. Mom and I need *Obaasan*. Even if her mind isn't all the way here, *she* is. And I—we—love her." Brander swallows hard, and I catch his feathery black eyelashes beating hard, like tiny butterflies trying to escape. "No matter what."

"So she really will be at the wedding? Your mom won't change her mind at the last minute?"

"Does she *look* like she's going to change her mind?" Brander gestures to the hospital bed, where both *Obaasan* and Midori are dozing, their chests rising and falling in near-perfect unison. From this vantage point, Midori seems small. Thin. Almost fragile. Definitely not the monster-in-law I'd made her out to be. "I think this is a turning point."

*Oh, dear God, let it be.*

# Chapter Twenty-Seven

*HELLO, SWEET GIRL,*

*Only one more day to go! How I wish I was there with you to breathe in the excitement. But I'm not, and there's no sense mourning the things that aren't—not on your special day. Don't make a fuss over me. Don't think about what could have been. Don't worry about anything other than having the best day of your life with the man you love the most...*

Oh, Mom.

Tears fill my eyes, and I fold the letter in two before I can finish reading. Jazz would have a fit if I showed up to the rehearsal with red-rimmed eyes and a drippy nose.

Instead of snuffling my way through the letter, I slip it into my shorts pocket to read later, then head downstairs, where Grams and Macie are busy in the kitchen. "What in the world is going on in here?" The entire kitchen smells like a cross between a fancy French bakery and a greasy spoon diner. "Are you making bacon?"

"For maple-bacon donuts." Macie nods so fast I can practically see her freshly straightened hair frizzing before my eyes. She tosses a piece of the ingredient in question to Zuzu, who snaps it up before going right back to hovering greedily underfoot. "Midori said she wanted a...how did she say it, Grams?"

Gramma closes her eyes for a moment, as if deep in thought. "Something along the lines of 'a varied selection of miniature desserts with a wide variety of flavor profiles'."

"Oh."

"In other words," Macie rolls an elastic off of her wrist and throws her hair into a ponytail. "We have to make a little bit of everything. It's going to be epic."

"We need all this on top of the cake?"

"The cake is for you and Brander. *This* is for the late-night dessert bar. In case people don't want—"

"Macie!" Gramma practically yelps the word right as the oven timer goes off with an earsplitting blare. "Remember..."

*Remember what?*

"Sorry, Grams." Macie puffs at a stray piece of hair as she races to the oven to rescue what appears to be a tray full of miniature meringue nests. "Shoo, Olive. Get out of here. You know I can't keep a secret."

"Isn't that the truth." I head out to the porch swing alone. Brander is busy with work—the day before his wedding, of all days—and Jazz and Midori are fussing over last-minute preparations. With Dad and Emily currently soaring high above the Pacific Ocean, headed for the Kahului airport, I'm out of luck. Not even Mango is around to keep me company. Since Brander and I are taking off on our honeymoon to France—with a little visit to England, aka the land of all things Jane Austen, thrown in—right after the wedding, Jazz volunteered to board her at the rescue until we got home.

*Okay, God. I guess it's You and me.*

I lean against the swing and pull my legs to my chin. Funny how, after tomorrow, there'll be no more sitting out here with a good book, waking up to the smell of muffins, or tripping over Macie's scruffy little food hound. The place I learned to call *home* will become *Gramma's house* once more. Tears burn in my eyes again. Not good.

*Think about Brander. Your new house. The wedding.*

*The wedding that Mom isn't going to be at.*

This isn't working.

I check the time on my phone—five hours until the rehearsal.

*Be still.*

The words come in a rush, a voice that is at once booming and silent. They echo in my chest and hum in my soul, ringing out like a clear, crystal bell.

*Be still.*

There it is again—a voice that's soft and strong like Mom's, yet, at the same time, deep and flowing. A voice that could come straight from Heaven...

Or my over-stressed, over-active imagination.

*Be still.*

Okay, then. *I'm listening, God.*

The breeze stirs the bushes around me, blowing my hair first this way, then that. Birds chitter and chatter in a neighbor's yard, and voices from the beach intermingle with the sporadic crashing of waves. Somehow, the place that I hated has become the one that my soul loves the most. And I'm so glad it has.

I don't know how long I sit there—thinking, praying, *being*—but I know that, when I open my eyes, I nearly fall off the swing.

"Mark?" I blink at my boss, who seems smaller than usual and definitely out-of-place standing on Gramma's porch. He's wearing shorts and an ill-fitting polo, like he's about to head out to the golf course. "This is a surprise."

He bares his teeth, revealing his usual mouthful of coffee-stained choppers, and holds out a wrapped gift. "I wanted to give you your wedding present."

A...wedding present? From Mark? "Um, thanks." I take the thin, flat package, and it nearly buckles under my grip. What did he get me, a stack of paper?

"Don't open it until you're told to." There's a strange glimmer in his eye that I don't quite recognize, but it's definitely not his usual money-hungry gleam. This looks more like...kindness. "Congratulations, Olive."

"Thanks."

He stands there for a second, shuffling his too-big feet, before turning to leave. And then, before he's out of earshot, I call out.

"The wedding's tomorrow on Ka'anapali beach. At sunset. You can come if you want."

With that, Mark's face lights up with a sort of joy I didn't know he could possibly exhibit. He flashes two fleshy thumbs up before folding himself into his car and taking off.

I stare after his car for a minute before turning my attention to the package. It's awkwardly wrapped, and none of the paper's edges are at all what you'd call straight, but there's a big, curly bow and a tag with my name on it. I bend the package, and it gives easily. Stationery, maybe?

I finger a loose piece of tape. I could peel it away and get a peek inside—Mark would never know. But he told me not to open it until I was supposed to, and there definitely isn't anyone telling me to open it.

Which means now there's one more secret hovering in the air.

The rehearsal is chaos.

The first time we run through the ceremony, Dad isn't even around to walk me down the aisle—he's stuck in traffic halfway between Kaanapali Beach and Kahului. By the time he and Emily arrive, it's half-dark and Jonah has managed to misplace his notes. He ends up performing the entire ceremony from memory, which means it's rough to say the least.

"Let's take a break already." Jazz motions to three extra-large boxes of Pirate Pete's pizza. Tonight, there's no pineapple to be found, thank goodness.

The break is short-lived, but at least it gives Jonah enough time to find his notes. Apparently, Hunter and Jazz thought it would be a riot to hide them under the marriage certificate. Jonah had other ideas.

"Ready?" Jonah takes his place at the front of the altar and claps his hands to silence the group, not that we're doing all that much talking—more like yawning, actually. "From the top!"

Jazz presses play on her phone, and the sound of ambient keyboard and fingerstyle ukulele pours out from the Delacroixs' fancy portable sound system. Brander gallantly escorts Midori to her seat, then lays a rose on the chair that's been left empty for Mom before joining Jonah at the altar.

"Wait, stop!" Gramma shoots up from her seat and waves a hanky in the air. Jazz presses pause, and the music cuts out. I lean around the staging area to get a better view.

"This isn't right." Grams extends one knobby finger, pointing at the chair that's been reserved for Mom.

"What?" Jazz squints at me from our hiding place behind the whitewashed panels that separate the staging area from the pampas-grass-lined aisle.

"Brander, take that chair away." Gramma points again to the chair, the one already trimmed with lace from Mom's wedding dress and the picture of her that usually hangs in

Gramma's hallway. "We all know Sophie would've hated for us to make a fuss over her."

"What?" Dad brushes past me and stalks down the aisle, gaping at Gramma the whole time. "I thought—"

"Better yet, don't take it away." Gramma pauses and draws in a deep breath, as if silently praying for the courage to deliver her next line, then lifts the picture frame and tucks it into her oversized tote bag. "Emily, why don't you sit here instead?"

"Me?" Emily lays a hand to her chest. "But—"

"Any friend of Alex's is a friend of mine. And, in Hawaii, our friends are our *ohana*. Our family."

"I wouldn't want anyone to assume—"

"What? That you're in love with my dad?" Macie jogs over to join Grams and Dad, arms knotted over her chest. "That's dumb. It's obvious you two are going to be the next to get hitched."

Jazz quirks an eyebrow at me, and we stifle our snickers as Dad and Emily stare at each other awkwardly.

I clear my throat. "Since you put it so delicately, Macie, I happen to think it's a great idea. Emily, would you be my stand-in mom tomorrow?"

"I—I..." Emily's eyes grow strangely bright, and I try not to flinch as she reaches out to hold Dad's hand. "I'd be absolutely honored. Are you sure?"

"Positive." Grams and I say it at the same time, both of us bobbing our heads. Must be genetic.

"Sophie was always happiest when she was behind the scenes. She wouldn't want a veritable monument to herself at her daughter's wedding." Dad clears his throat. "But Olive, this is your special day. Are you sure—"

"Dad, seriously." I step closer and take his and Emily's

hands. "I know this is what Mom would want. In fact..."

I reach deep into my pocket and pull out Mom's letter from this morning. "I have it in writing from Mom that she doesn't want us making a fuss. Emily, that chair is yours."

At that, both of them break into bright, beaming smiles, like the sun has finally broken through the clouds after a rainy day.

*Perfect.*

"Now, may I have the rings?" Jonah's official, pastor-mode voice makes him sound older. More professional. So different from the surfer-dude youth leader I've come to know him as.

"We're really doing this, aren't we?" I whisper to Brander as Hunter mimes giving Jonah the rings.

"Doing what? Getting married?" One corner of Brander's mouth quirks up even higher than the other—which is saying something, since he's already grinning.

And then...

Brander gets a gleam in his eyes—a wicked twinkle that makes me wonder if I've fallen prey to a practical joke.

"What? Do I have cheese on my chin?" *And, if so, why didn't you tell me* before *we started the rehearsal?*

Brander's smile grows even wider, if such a thing is possible. "Close your eyes."

"O*kay.*"

"Hold out your hand."

Brander releases his grip, and I do as I'm told. "This isn't going to be part of the ceremony tomorrow, is it?"

The only response is a sudden clinking. Something metallic drops into my palm.

"What is it?" It's too heavy to be a ring, and it isn't shaped right either. It feels almost like...

I open my eyes. "A key?"

Two keys, actually. One small, serviceable and worn, the other shinier. Brighter. *New.*

I turn to Brander as Jazz steps forward to hand him something—the same clumsily-wrapped package that Mark gave me earlier.

"I think it's time to open this." Brander quickly rips off the wrapping and pulls out...

"A magazine?"

"An early copy of the latest edition of the *West Maui Sun*, to be exact. See the cover story?" Brander holds up the magazine. On the cover is a picture of a couple sitting on the beach, sharing a shave ice. *Of course.* But...wait.

"Is that us?" I peer closer. "Who took this? And when?"

"A spy." Jazz smirks at Hunter.

He raises his arms, as if in defense. "I couldn't turn down a chance to break out the old telephoto lens."

"But what are we doing on the cover of the *West Maui Sun?*"

"Let's see." Brander opens the magazine, flips through a few pages, then hands it to Jonah. "Would you do the honors?"

"Sure thing." Jonah clears his throat and begins to read. "Shave Ice and a Side of Aloha, by Olive Galloway."

"What?" I shake my head. "Mark told me I was off the case. I never even proofread that article. And what about—"

"Shh." Brander brings a finger to my lips. "Listen."

Jonah reads aloud, his big, booming pastor voice rising and falling over the words of the article—words I'd written, about Hank's unfailing love and his selfless desire to serve both his wife and the community.

But, instead of ending after my concluding paragraph, Jonah keeps reading. "When August Delacroix, owner and CEO of Delacroix Hospitality, heard about the tragedy, he and his son, a local music sensation, stepped in to help. Along with providing for the long-term care of Mr. Murphy's wife, Delacroix purchased the Shave Ice Shack and plans to keep it running under the umbrella of his resort properties and other tourist experiences. We spoke with Delacroix's son, who said—"

"I'm excited about this new chapter in the life of the Shave Ice Shack. And, as the new business manager, I can't wait to continue spreading the aloha spirit to kamaʻāina and visitors alike." Brander recites the words, as if from memory, and lifts the keys from my hand. "Olive, when we say I do tomorrow, I'm not only going to be giving you the key to my heart—I'm also asking you to join me in this journey. Do you think you could stand taking a shift at the Shave Ice Shack with me again?"

"Are you kidding?" I peer into Brander's face, searching his familiar features for any sign of a prank or practical joke. There isn't one—and this is such a serious matter that I doubt Brander would joke about it anyway. "You're not kidding, are you? You mean—you're serious?"

"Meet the new manager of the Shave Ice Shack." Hunter steps forward and claps Brander on the back, and then suddenly we're all hugging and laughing and talking, and somewhere off in the distance Dad is explaining to Emily exactly what the Shave Ice Shack is and why it's so important.

And then somehow, with a bunch of happy tears and excited giggles, we finish the rehearsal, and everyone is gone—except for Brander, Jazz, and Hunter.

"You own the Shave Ice Shack now." I shake my head at Brander. "I've gotta say, it's a better fit for you than working in an office all day."

"Technically my dad owns it, but yeah. I officially resigned from my management position last month, and Dad rehired me under their food and beverage department. My paycheck is a little slimmer now, but—"

"But you're the manager of the Shave Ice Shack." Jazz practically swoons. "Does that mean I get shave ice for free from now on?"

"Not a chance. But free refills? Every time."

"Score!" Jazz pumps her arms, and she shares a look with Hunter. "Can you take me home? I still have to iron my dress for tomorrow, and besides—the lovebirds could use some alone time."

This time, though, I can't help but wonder which two *lovebirds* she's referring to. As Jazz and Hunter disappear into the fading twilight, Brander wraps me in his arms. "Are you sure you're happy?"

"Happier than I've ever been in my life."

"I wanted to tell you about all of this at our last counseling session, but Jazz and Hunter convinced me to keep it a surprise."

"You pulled it off. Spectacularly." I rest my head on his chest, the steady, sturdy beating of his heart thudding in my ear like a promise of things to come. "I wonder what they have cooked up for tomorrow."

"Well..." Brander lifts a finger to trace the outline of my jaw before pressing a kiss to my lips. "I suppose there's only one way to find out. Let's get you home. Tomorrow will be here before we know it."

*And it can't come a moment too soon.*

# Chapter Twenty-Eight

"GUYS, WE'RE GONNA BE *LATE*!" MACIE thuds up the stairs, her blue-and-white dip-dyed bridesmaid dress flowing behind her in a whirlwind of silk and chiffon as she bursts into our bedroom-turned-dressing room. "The wedding starts in two hours and I haven't even straightened my hair!"

"Then get straightening," Jazz mumbles around a mouthful of hairpins. I watch in Gramma's giant, tacky, mirrored closet door as Jazz secures another strand of my flyaway driftwood-colored hair. "I'm all ready...and so is Olive. Voila!" Jazz spritzes my hair—which, for once looks like something other than a massive mass of tangles—with a final blast of hairspray, then motions for me to stand.

"My big sister, all grown up." Macie gives a dramatic sniff and mimes wiping her eyes, but there's an honest-to-goodness catch in her voice all the same.

"Oh, come here." I pull Jazz and Macie in for a hug that lasts for one long, delicious moment of sisterhood—until Jazz pulls away and waves a finger at me.

"Quit it, or you'll mess up your dress. Or knowing you, you'll start crying and your makeup will run everywhere and, we'll have to start all over."

"And then we really *will* be late." Macie stalks over to the desk, which has been transformed into an impromptu hair-and-make-up counter. "Now let me straighten my hair."

She picks up the iron and is about to clamp it down on one of her springy curls when I pull it out of her hand. "Hey!"

Macie shoots me a glare. "We don't have a lot of time. Straightening my hair takes *forever.*"

"Why don't you leave it curly? Like you used to?" I plead with my eyes, wrinkling up my forehead and giving her my best imitation of Zuzu's pouty puppy-dog look. "It's cute. And...it's *you.*"

"I don't want it to look like it used to." Macie crosses her arms over her dress. "*Nothing* is going to be the same anymore, so why shouldn't I change my hair?" The words are flippant—borderline rude. If Gramma had caught wind of them, she'd already be halfway through a lecture on respect. Or...

Maybe she'd understand.

"Come with me, Mace." I drag my sister into the hallway, down the stairs, and through the front door before plopping onto the porch swing, careful not to snag my wedding dress on the splintery back.

"What are you *doing*?" Macie stares at me like I've sprouted a horn on my head instead of a veil. "You know it's almost time to go."

"I know, but listen...Macie." I gulp in a breath. How can I explain to her that, even though everything is about to change, that doesn't mean that things between us can't still be the same? "I'm the worst at this heart-to-heart stuff."

"Hire Jazz as a translator." Macie shrugs. There's that tone again—half exasperation, half something else. Something deeper...something that hurts?

"Macie, look at me."

She turns her head just enough to squint at me out of the corner of her eye. "You're going to be late to your own wedding if you don't spit it out."

"Fine then. I love you."

Macie scrunches her nose. "Isn't that what you're supposed to say to Brander?"

"Yeah, but—"

"That's the problem. You love him so much you aren't going to have any room left in your life for little-old me. Trust me, Kanani's big sister got married last year. I know how these things work. You're going to go off to happy-honeymoon land and forget about the rest of the *world*."

I snort. "I am *not* Kanani's big sister. And you're not Kanani—you're Macie. No matter what, you're my sister. One of my very best friends."

"But I'm going to come in second place." Something shimmers in the corner of Macie's eye. "Forever."

"Macie..." I blow out a stream of breath, long and slow, as everything that's in my heart manages to arrange itself into something resembling coherency. "There is no second place. Or first place or *any* place, for that matter."

"But doesn't Brander—"

"Come first? Yeah, in some ways I guess he does. But not in my heart. Hearts don't work that way—there is no first place or last place. There's just love. Love you can give to *everyone* all the time. No matter where I am or how much I love Brander, that doesn't lessen the way I feel about you. You're my sister—you, Macie Galloway. Not Brander or Gramma or Jazz or anyone else. We're sisters. Built-in friends forever. Nothing will ever change that."

"But things are just going to be so *weird*. You won't live here anymore."

"No, but I'll come over and visit. And come on—don't tell me you aren't at least a *teensy* bit excited about getting to have your own room."

A sliver of a grin slides onto Macie's face. "Busted."

With that, we burst out laughing. Somehow that laughing turns to hugging and hugging turns to—

*Not yet.*

I swallow against a sudden lump in my throat. There will be plenty of time for happy tears later. Right now, I have a wedding to get ready for.

"I still want to straighten my hair though," Macie grumbles as we head back upstairs, running through a list of reasons why she should fry her entire mop-top in the name of beauty.

"You're sure you don't want to go natural? It looks way better on you," I protest one last time as we step back into the bedroom-turned-beauty-parlor.

"She's right, Mace. Let me see." Jazz steps over from where she's been shining the metal pole of her prosthesis, grabs a jar of hair gel, and starts combing it through Macie's mop, turning every cockeyed kink in it into a perfectly styled curl. "Even if you spend an hour on your hair, it's going to frizz the second you step outside. You should...you know. Be yourself."

Jazz winks at me over Macie's head, and I lend her a smile in return.

Something tells me that those words run deeper than a bit of offhanded advice from one bridesmaid to another—that, whether she realizes it or not, Jazz is reminding herself of the very same thing.

"That's what we all need to do, really." I speak the words almost to myself, but somehow they come out louder than I'd intended.

"What do you mean?" Jazz peers at me over Macie's mop of curls, where she's expertly twisting a braid around the front of Macie's head like a crown.

"None of us are perfect—but God is. And He loves us

through it all. He wants *our hearts*." I might as well be standing on a soapbox or behind a preacher's pulpit, but something—the joy in my heart, the anticipation of the ceremony, or something from above—keeps me going. "That's why they call us the bride of Christ. Because true love never fails—and neither does God."

Jazz stares at me, her wide silver eyes shimmering. "You're exactly right, Olive." She stares at the ground—or a certain prosthesis, maybe. The fancy custom-made cosmetic leg Midori ordered didn't come in time, and though Jazz hasn't said anything, something tells me that it's bugging her.

Just a little.

"You're beautiful, Jazz," I whisper. Because she is. And then, before the whole moment can grow so soggy and sappy that we all end up crying before it's time, I waggle my brows. "I know someone else who thinks so too."

"Oh, stop." Jazz pitches a hairbrush at me, and I barely duck in time to send it sailing over my head.

*Wait until you catch that bouquet.* A smirk tries to break through onto my face, but I swallow it and reach for the embellished handbag that Midori had custom-made for me. Its lacy flowers and delicate pearlescent beads once adorned Mom's own wedding dress, but now, they've found a new life decorating the simple white clutch. It's loaded with wedding-day essentials, including a lacy handkerchief from Gramma—for happy tears, so she says—and Emily's silver sixpence. Different things from different people. Some of them family, some of them friends.

All of them ohana.

*I miss you, Mom.*

"Olive!" Jazz's voice snaps through my reverie before I can get teary-eyed again, and she tosses me my pair of fancy *slippas* with lacy straps. "Get your shoes on. It's time to go."

"Olive!" Gramma races down the front steps and presses a black velvet box tied with a satin bow into my hand before the limo—yes, a limo—that Midori hired for the day can sweep Jazz, Macie, and me away to the spot on the beach where I'll be walking down the aisle. "I almost forgot! This is for you."

"Who's it from?"

"A handsome young man dropped it off this morning." Gramma's laugh lines bunch together on either side of her face.

I study the box and tug at the crisp white bow, but Jazz practically pushes me into the car before I can open it. Macie piles in after us and immediately checks the mini fridge.

"Cool, they have sodas!" She snaps the lid on one and takes a long swig.

Jazz follows suit, and I scoot into the farthest seat before tugging at the bow and opening the tiny box.

A note—

*I can't wait to write our story together.*

*Love, Brander.*

Inside is a necklace made up of a cluster of nine diamonds, all of a different shape and size. I hold it up to the light and it glimmers, the precious stones winking at me. Laughing. Beckoning me to embark on this new, Spirit-led adventure.

*God, You know how excited I am to start this new chapter, but You know what? I'm only human, and I'm not the best writer in the world. Why don't You handle this one?*

Because, no matter where God leads, I know that Brander and I are going to follow.

Together.

# Chapter Twenty-Nine ·

IT ALL GOES BY IN A BLUR—to have and to hold, for richer, for poorer, until death do us part. I stand in front of Brander, staring into his warm, almond-shaped eyes. The low-hanging sun casts its magical golden rays over everyone I love as we witness this magic moment.

*Together.*

True to Midori's word, *Obaasan* has a place of honor next to her daughter. They sit together, watching the ceremony, sniffling, and dabbing at their eyes with matching embroidered hankies—ones that I bought just for them. *Obaasan's* mind could be here or it could be floating off somewhere in the past, but what matters right now is that she and Midori are here.

*Together.*

Another band of white gold, one rimmed with a halo of tiny, delicate diamonds, joins the ring on my finger. When Jonah finally says those five magical words, "you may kiss the bride," it's as if God orchestrates it Himself—or maybe Mom pulls a few strings up in heaven—because the sun slips behind the horizon just as my lips meet Brander's for our first kiss as husband and wife.

*Together.*

A million hugs, kisses, and photos later, Brander, Jazz, Hunter, and I are alone on the beach. The others have caravanned down the path to the resort, where what's sure to be the wedding reception of the century is already in full swing, but the four of us are left behind, soaking in this magical, blissful moment.

Hunter cut his hair for the big day—the manbun is gone—and Jazz sneaks an extra peek at him as we stand together amid the crashing waves. Could it be that she's falling under the spell of a cute guy in a spiffy suit? If so, Hunter, would be too smitten to even notice.

"I guess we should go." Brander is finally the one to speak, his voice at once soft and rough, as if his throat is full of happy tears that he doesn't quite know what to do with. Of course, I would only know that because my own voice sounds the same way.

"Right. We should."

None of us move.

We stand, waded up to our ankles in the water, together. An evening breeze whispers through the palm trees, tugging at strands of my hair. Brander's fingers lace into mine, the smooth band of his koa wood wedding ring gliding across my hand. Up and down the beach, tiki torches flicker.

"It's so perfect I could...I could..." I sniff.

"For heaven's sake, don't *cry*! We need to go eat. But first..." Jazz pulls something out of her handbag.

A lighter.

She flicks it on and off, a flame wiggling in the slight breeze. "First it's time for a little fire."

"I cannot *believe* that you actually did that." I shake my head at Jazz over Midori's catered sushi-and-Hawaiian-barbecue dinner—and here I'd seriously thought that I'd get stuck eating foie gras.

"I applaud you." Brander ducks his head, cheeks still pink. Though whether it's from the warm of Jazz and Hunter's surprise bonfire or mortification over actually dumping in that entire box of girls' phone numbers I'm not sure. "I didn't think you'd have the guts to pull it off."

"Wow, that stings." Jazz rubs her shoulder, as though Brander's words have wounded more than her ego. "I thought you'd have more confidence in me than that."

"Fair enough." Brander lifts his chopsticks to take another bite of yellowtail sashimi when the speaker closest to us crackles and the DJ cuts the music.

"Who's ready to *par-taaay*?" He's enthusiastic to the point of being obnoxious, and I practically cringe in my chair. Where on earth did Midori dig him up?

Hunter and Jazz don't seem to mind though, because they join a handful of other party-hardy guests on the dance floor as the DJ gets them started on the electric slide.

"We don't have to do that whole first dance thing, do we?" I cut my eyes at the dance floor, where I'd be more likely to bust an ankle or shinbone than any sort of a move.

"Nope." Brander shakes his head. "Mom knows we don't dance."

I pretend to breathe a sigh of relief, then reach into my clutch and pull out a tiny box. "Here. Before they come back—open it."

The box fits snugly in the palm of Brander's hand—there isn't much in there anyway—and he makes quick work of the tiny package.

Inside, lies a brushed bronze guitar pick with a tiny heart punched out of the tip, nestled beneath a custom engraving—*to the moon and back.*

Brander traces the words with his finger, then looks up to meet my gaze.

"You know I do, right? Love you, that is. I can't imagine sitting here with anyone else right now."

"Even Mr. Darcy?" Brander winks, then nods to Midori's *Pride-and-Prejudice*-meets-beach-wedding decor scheme, a far cry from the glittery, glitzy, and glamorous soirée I'd been preparing myself for.

"Not even Mr. Darcy." I steal a quick kiss when no one is looking before taking a last bite of dinner. "Face it, Brander Delacroix. You're stuck with me."

"For life?"

"For life."

# Chapter Thirty

THE PARTY LASTS LONG INTO the night, and a full canopy of stars has covered the sky by the time Brander and I cut the cake—delicious—and Jazz and Hunter give their speeches—hilarious, as anticipated.

Around ten o'clock, Grams and Macie lay out their dessert buffet alongside a cart with a pinstriped awning and the words *The Shave Ice Shack* hand-lettered across the front. "A new marketing idea," Brander whispers to me before cutting to the front of the line to get us a jumbo cone of the shack's famous wedding cake flavor.

"We'll roll this along the Ka'anapali beach walk giving out mini sample cones—and blessing a whole bunch of people while we're at it." Brander hands me a spoon. "*Tutu* made the sign."

A tiny piece of me melts, just like the ice on my spoon. "I still can't believe that you did this—and that Hank said yes. And that—" Brander pops a spoonful of shave ice in my mouth before I can say any more. *Yum.* It's sweet and buttery and cake-flavored all at once. But it could never be as sweet as the kiss that follows.

"Guys, come on!" Macie races over to us, her chocolatey curls flying all around her face. "It's time for Olive to throw the bouquet!"

*This is it.* I catch Gramma's eye across the patio and waggle my eyebrows at her. Grams turns to whisper to Emily, who whispers to Midori, who looks like she's actually having *fun.*

The single ladies—including Emily, Macie, and Jazz—cluster together in the middle of the dance floor. I sneak a peek at the group as I prepare to throw my bundle of massive peach-and-white flowers and seeded eucalyptus. My plan must be working because Jazz is smack dab in the center.

And with Macie on one side and Emily on the other, there's no way she's going anywhere soon.

I close my eyes and lean forward over the bouquet, letting the cascading greenery sway in the breeze for a moment. With the wind in my hair and the sound of the waves in my ears, I find myself praying. Not only for Jazz and Hunter and whatever kind of future God has planned for them, but also for Emily and Macie and all of the other girls out on that dance floor.

*That someday they could have the kind of love Brander and I share.*

Then I lift my arms and heaving the bouquet—it's heavier than I'd imagined—over my head. I turn in time to watch it sail across the dance floor. Farther...farther...

"Oh, yeah!" Macie pumps her fist as the bouquet hits Jazz almost square in the chest. "Great catch, Jazz!"

"But I—I didn't. I mean—" Jazz's eyes are wide and directed at a certain someone who's standing on the sidelines, hands in his pockets, eyes wide. "Macie, that was totally meant for you. Come on, take it."

"No way." Macie sticks out her tongue and shoves the bouquet back into Jazz's arms. "Besides, I can't be the next to married—it would take me ten years, at least. You'd be an old maid by then. This is all yours, Jazz."

I can't quite hear her response over the din of the other

partygoers, but it sure looks to me like Jazz mutters something akin to "thanks a lot" under her breath before taking the bouquet, exiting the dance floor, and bumping right into Hunter.

*Impeccable timing.*

Let's hope that, while Brander and I are exploring the streets of England and lavender fields of French Provence on our honeymoon, Jazz and Hunter can be keeping each other company.

"You ready to go?" Brander appears at my side, his sky-blue linen tie loosened around the collar of his white dress shirt. His beige linen jacket disappeared long ago, and it looks like he's even kicked off his retro-style suede shoes in favor of a pair of more comfortable slippas.

"Ready as I'll ever be."

I take his hand and we exit to a display of fireworks above and handheld sparklers below. Everyone cheers, and Brander and I make a run for it as Jazz, Macie, Hunter, and the others do their best to pelt us with heart-shaped confetti cut from vintage book pages.

Fireworks thunder overhead, raining down in a dazzling display of silver and gold, as Brander and I race down the path to where his Porsche is waiting, decked out in a slightly-too-flashy "just married" banner and a garland of eucalyptus leaves.

Almost before I know what's happening, Brander throws open the passenger door, sweeps me off my feet, and nestles me in the front seat before running around to the drivers' side. "Away we go," he shouts over the commotion of well-wishers and fireworks. He fires up the car and puts it in drive before leaning over to give me another kiss—one that holds a whisper of all that's yet to come.

I kiss him back, promising him all of my love—my *aloha*—until the day I die. And then...

We're gone, driving off into the dark, racing evermore toward our future.

*Together.*

# Author's Note

They say that the Lord has a sense of humor, and boy, does He ever!

When I started writing this book, I never could have imagined that God was busy writing my own real-life love story. But, as I toiled away at the first draft of *Promise Me Aloha* and prayed about my own future, I began to realize that the Lord had *two* love stories for me to write. And one of them was about to leap off the page and become reality.

I wasn't looking for love—hadn't even considered the possibility of dating. Bookish boyfriends like Jo March's Professor Bhaer were more than enough to keep me company as I worked on my books and finished my bachelor's degree. But Elias LaLande, my very own Brander Delacroix, stepped into the pages of my life when I was least expecting it. Sitting only a few pews away from each other every Sunday in church, we'd known each other in passing for years. But through coffee-not-coffee dates and hours spent discussing the merits of some of literature's greatest classics, I realized that God had brought us together for a special reason. Even when falling in love was the farthest thing from my mind.

It just goes to show—the Lord has an amazing plan for each and every one of us. As I worked to give Olive and Brander the happily ever after they deserved, God was giving me one of my own. I was knee-deep in edits one springtime afternoon when Elias and I went on a surprise adventure that ended with him dropping to one knee and asking me to marry him.

I, of course, said yes.

The real-life version of Olive's ring found its way onto my finger, cake was eaten, and hugs were exchanged as we celebrated the beauty of God's perfect will in our lives.

No matter what season we're in, we should never forget that the Lord has incredible things planned for us. He is the author of our whole life story and, with Him guiding our journey, it's sure to be fantastic. I don't know what the future holds for me, but I know God does, and I'm excited to come along for the ride.

If you'd like to follow along with me on my writing *and* wedding journey, go ahead and give me a follow on Instagram @taylor.bennett.author or via my newsletter at: taylor--bennett.com/contact/my-newsletter.

Until I Write Again,
Taylor

# Discussion Questions

1. Several years have passed since the last Tradewinds book. What do you think of Olive, Brander, and Jazz's career choices? Do you think these occupations are a good fit for their personalities?

2. Macie appears to be well on her way to becoming a moody teenager. Do you think her attitude was justifiable, considering the massive changes in her own life? Have you ever had to handle a sibling with a similar attitude? How did you feel about it?

3. After years as a widower, Olive's dad is finally dating again! Were you surprised by this revelation? Do you feel that Olive had a right to be suspicious of Emily at first? Have you had a similar experience? How did you handle it?

4. Hank decides that keeping the Shave Ice Shack open isn't worth taking time away from his wife, even though she begs him not to shut it down for her sake. What would you have wanted Hank to do if you were his wife? Have you or a close friend ever been in a similar situation, where your entire world was turned upside down, and you had to make a life-changing choice? What helped you during that time?

5. In this story, Jazz struggles more to accept her appearance than she has in previous books. Do you think this has anything to do with her growing interest in Hunter? Do you ever feel insecure about your own body? What do you think about Jazz's challenge to "be yourself?"

6. While in Las Vegas, Jazz decides to get a tattoo! Do you agree with her choice? If you were going to get a meaningful tattoo somewhere, what would it look like? What would it say?

7. At first, Olive and Midori struggle to combine their ideas into a wedding that reflects both of their original visions. Do you think that Olive's ceremony/reception compromise was fair? Have you ever had to make a major compromise with a family member? How did it turn out?

# Recipe

Take a bite out of Olive's love story—and my own! Not only is this cake served at Olive's wedding, but it's also the exact kind that I indulged in while celebrating my own engagement. Have I mentioned that cake is my love language? This recipe one is one of my favorites. The honey-mascarpone icing takes cream cheese frosting to a whole new level, and the light floral notes in the lavender brittle never fail to remind me of Maui's famous Ali'i Kula Lavender farm. Yum!

Honey-Lavender Cake
1 box of yellow cake mix (or your own favorite flavor)
Honey-Mascarpone Icing
Lavender Brittle
1. Prepare the boxed mix as directed, pouring into two 9" cake pans and baking until done.
2. Frost layers with honey-mascarpone icing, topping with lavender brittle as desired.
3. Eat and enjoy!!

Honey-Mascarpone Icing
1/4 cup butter, softened
8 oz. mascarpone cheese, softened
1/4 cup honey
1/8 tsp. salt
16 oz powdered sugar
1. Beat butter with an electric mixer until creamy, then add mascarpone, honey, and salt and beat until combined.
2. Add powdered sugar little by little, beating at a lower speed until blended.
3. Increase mixer speed and whip until creamy

Lavender Brittle

1 cup sugar

1 1/2 tsp. Culinary lavender

1. Line a baking sheet with parchment paper and coat with cooking spray.

2. Combine sugar and 1/2 cup water in a small saucepan, cooking over medium-high heat and stirring gently until sugar dissolves.

3. Cook without stirring for 5 minutes or until golden in color.

4. Remove mixture from heat and stir in lavender.

5. Spread the mixture onto a prepared baking sheet and let cool completely before breaking into pieces.

Enjoy!

CPSIA information can be obtained
at www.ICGtesting.com
Printed in the USA
LVHW011915111222
735004LV00005B/517